This book is dedicated in loving memory of:
Anne and Frank Shook
Thomas Richard Shook
Gerti and Alfred Strauss
Susan Strauss Lipschutz

Search for the Sacred Scroll

Book 2: The Secret of the Crowns

Mark Leslie Shook

Newhouse Creative Group

NCG Key

"It is...clearer than the sun at noon that the Pentateuch was not written by Moses, but by someone who lived long after Moses." – Benedictus Spinoza, *Tractatus Theologico-Politicus, 1670 CE*

Map by Matthew Thomas

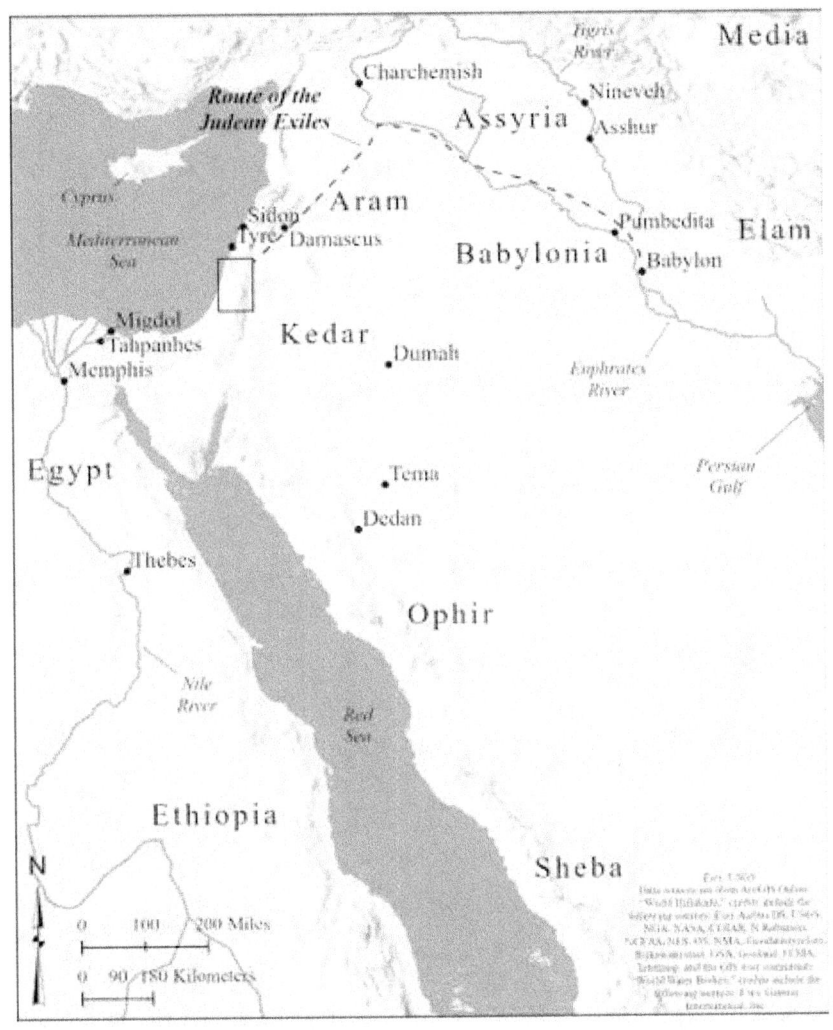

Map by Matthew Thomas

CHAPTER ONE

DATE: March 17, 2009
TIME: 10:30 A.M. Local Time
PLACE: Trauma Unit, Souraski Medical Center, Tel Aviv

Marine Gunnery Sergeant Aaron Keller was struggling. All of the images in his head were jumbled together. The sounds and voices he heard made absolutely no sense. One moment he was advising a company of Iraqi Police in Fallujah. The next, he was landing on an aircraft carrier in the Mediterranean. The scenes kept switching without warning, like someone operating a remote going quickly from channel to channel, switching from sports to news to drama and back again. Two of the images, with their sounds, were terrifying. They kept repeating. In the first, he was ambushed on a deserted street in Fallujah. In the second, he was blown up and thrown out of a tea shop, onto a street in Israel. Am I in Israel? What, in God's name am I doing in Israel? What is that ringing in my ears? I must open my eyes, he thought. It's the only way I can end this nightmare.

"Welcome back to the land of the living, Sergeant."

Keller barely heard the voice over the ringing in his ears. It was muffled as if spoken through a thick towel. His eyes slowly opened and adjusted to the soft light. He was in a bed, maybe a bed in a hospital room. Not much color. Muted sounds. Standing next to the bed wearing surgical scrubs, there was a man with dark skin and a road map of wrinkles on his face.

Keller tried to lift himself up and failed. He heard his voice asking as if from a distance. "Are you a doctor?"

"Sergeant, you and I just survived a terrorist bomb. My clothes were shredded in the explosion. The hospital gave me these scrubs to wear. I am Professor Shlomo Malik. Do you remember coming to see me with Rabbi Abby Stone?"

Keller shook his head. "I see your lips moving, but I can hardly hear you. What day is today? How long have I been here?"

Malik pointed to a calendar attached to a whiteboard by the bedside. He then pointed to the clock on the wall. He exaggerated his mouth movements to help Keller understand him. "Today is Tuesday, March 17. It's about 10:30 in the morning. You have been here, in this hospital, since the bomb exploded on Sunday afternoon, nearly two days ago. The doctor told me that the explosion has temporarily affected your hearing. It will clear up in time."

Keller's memory returned in a rush of sounds and images. This time, he succeeded in rising from his pillow. "Oh my God! Rabbi Stone! Is she alive? Is she all right?" He moved to get out of bed, only to find himself tethered to an IV pole with a needle in his arm.

Malik placed a restraining hand on Keller's shoulder. He continued to exaggerate his lip movements to assist Keller's comprehension. "Rabbi Stone is alive. She is being cared for in the ICU. This hospital is one of the best trauma centers in the world. The initial report is that her injuries are not life-threatening. She is in the ICU as a precaution. Now, lay back and try to slow down." He smiled. "Aside of some cuts and bruises, and a mild concussion, you are amazingly lucky. As am I."

Keller looked at Malik, who showed no visible injuries. "A bomb? What is this all about?"

"We were hit with shrapnel. Right now, infection is what concerns the doctors. Your IV is filled with antibiotics. You will have the tether for a while. Join the club." Malik pulled his own IV pole forward.

Keller rasped, "I need to see Rabbi Stone, now!"

Shaking his head, Malik continued, "Abby's trauma nurse told me we can see her as soon as her wounds are redressed. In the meantime, while we wait, tell me what you remember."

Keller searched his memory. "I found an ancient scroll... in Fallujah. Rabbi Stone and I brought the scroll to an archeologist in Jerusalem, one of her former teachers."

Malik came closer to the bed. "That was Daniel Carlson."

Keller tried to clear his throat. "Can you get me some water?"

Malik stepped over to the wheeled table next to the bed and poured water from a Styrofoam pitcher into a cup with a straw.

Keller drank slowly, trying to remember. "Thanks. That's much better," he said. "I remember Rabbi Stone wanted someone familiar with the Jews of Iraq to examine the scroll." He looked hard at Malik. "You! We were driving to Tel Aviv to meet you...we were nearly run off the road by some maniac driving a dump truck?" He shivered at the image of the truck smashing into their car and nearly throwing them off a cliff. "The police pulled us from the edge. After they questioned us, we went to your class at Tel Aviv University, then to your office at the museum."

Malik nodded. "Your memory is good."

Keller frowned. "You started examining a copy of the scroll. You were excited. You called it the 'Ezra Scroll.'" He closed his eyes, trying to put things together. He opened them again, an accusing look on his face. "You asked us to join you for tea. It was some hole-in-the-wall shop near the museum. That's when all hell broke loose." He snarled, "What happened to that copy? The actual scroll was stolen. I remember that now." Keller's voice rose, "The copy, where is it?"

Malik frowned. "Calm yourself, Sergeant. I would never let that copy out of my sight. I hid it before the medics got to me. I have it here." He patted his stomach.

"You ate it?"

Malik smiled. "Your injuries are more serious than I thought. No, I tucked the copy into the waistband of my scrubs. It is safe, for now."

Keller breathed a sigh of relief.

Malik leaned closer. "I need to tell you. I fear we are going to be interrogated by very interested parties. We need to get our stories straight."

"I have nothing to hide."

"If you want to continue investigating your discovery, you had better come up with a story that reveals as little as possible." Malik looked thoughtful. "It may be necessary to enlist some help from my special friends to locate and recover the original scroll."

Special friends? Keller fell back on the hospital bed. Malik had led them to the tea shop. He was hurt when the bomb went off, so he should not be a suspect. Were his wounds serious enough to cross him off the list? Was Malik to be trusted? Who could he trust after these 'accidents' that nearly took Abby and his life?

CHAPTER TWO

DATE: Fourth Day of the Third Month, In the Third Year Since The Destruction of Jerusalem
TIME: One Hour Before Noon
PLACE: The Home of Talmon ben Aram

Shoshana and Eli were destined to fall in love with each other. During the three years since his arrival in Samaria, their shared experience of surviving the trek across the desert brought them closer together. Their needling of one another, mostly based on their different tribal identities, had grown humorous, a sign of their growing affection. They had come to realize that their differences made them stronger.

"Open your eyes, Talmon. The Judean has feelings for Shoshana." Assiya, Shoshana's father's sister, expressed aloud what Talmon already knew. This was not the first time she instigated this conversation. But it was the first time that Talmon revealed what his thinking was about this delicate subject. "It is time for them to marry," Talmon said, deep in thought.

"What? Do you know what you are saying? A daughter of our people may not marry a Judean. If she did, you will no longer be *Melekh Shomron*, the ruler of Samaria."

"Sister, you are wise in most things. Wisdom comes to you from our mother. You wear it well as she did. It becomes you. But sometimes, wisdom is not enough. Sometimes courage must overtake wisdom."

"Not in this matter. Courage will lead to disaster. If the Bavlim who rule over us, hear that you have given your daughter to a Judean, they will suspect you have larger ambitions of uniting our people—"

"I can't control what the Bavlim suspect. But I am charged with the safety of our people—"

"And this is how you protect us? By provoking them?"

"The elders and I have discussed this matter many times. It is not the Bavlim we must fear. It is the Egyptians that will destroy us."

"I have heard the Bavlim boast of making the Nile a river of Bavel. We have seen what their armies can do. Egypt will be crushed by them," Assiya said.

"Perhaps, at first. But Egypt is a long way from Bavel. This is the greatest weakness of the Bavlim. They must supply their armies from here. That means they must have peace in Judea and Samaria. The Bavli Governor of this province told me as much last week. He confided that he was looking for a local *melekh* capable of keeping the peace between all the peoples of this land. I told him that I'm the *melekh* he is looking for."

"Your pride will get us all killed. How does Shoshana marrying the Judean ensure our safety?"

"He has a name, my sister. Eli also has earned the respect of our people and the Judeans. By joining Samaritan and Judean within my own family, I will have demonstrated my ability to maintain the peace in this land."

"This is a dangerous game that you are playing, brother. I hope you are right."

Talmon smiled, but also hoped he was doing the right thing for his daughter.

***

Four weeks later, Eli and Shoshana were married. The wedding should have been a joyous affair, but the pall of Jerusalem's destruction cast its shadow over the nearly four hundred Judean exiles in Samaria. There was no dancing, no music, and very little wine. No wedding so soon after the destruction of Jerusalem and the Sacred House could compensate for the loss of the Judeans' spiritual heart, their holy city.

At the ceremony's conclusion, Talmon sought out Azariah, the Judean Chief Priest. "I am deeply grateful that you stood in as Eli's father beneath the canopy and prepared the wedding contract. It meant a great deal to him."

Azariah bowed to Talmon. "My lord *Melekh*, you have graciously permitted us to dwell among your people in safety. This marriage is an important step in bringing Samaritans and Judeans closer to one another."

Talmon glanced at his daughter and Eli. "In their marriage, my friend, I see hope for the future."

Azariah replied, "May God hear our prayers."

After the wedding, Talmon presented the newlyweds with a house in the village. Eli thought the stone hut was not much larger than the one in which he was imprisoned when he arrived in Samaria. But from the moment they crossed the threshold, Shoshana demonstrated great skill in making it feel as if it was truly theirs.

Full of anticipation, Eli felt he was woefully unprepared for his first sexual experience. This subject was never discussed in the school for scribes. It certainly did not come up in conversation with his father. He knew what was expected but grew increasingly anxious as the hour approached.

Shoshana, on the other hand, had received detailed and practical lessons in marital matters from her father's wives. She knew what to do and when to do it.

Eli found their first night together a pleasant surprise and credited himself for the ease with which they consummated their union.

Shoshana was content to not needle him about her superiority in some matters. Unlike Eli, she understood that this marriage had a significance much greater than just their happiness. She knew the fate of her father and the future of their people rested on the unlikely love of a Judean scribe for a Samaritan woman.

CHAPTER THREE

DATE: March 17, 2009
TIME: 11:30 A. M. Local Time
PLACE: Trauma Unit, Souraski Medical Center, Tel Aviv

The sound of a sliding door slowly gliding in its track brought Rabbi Abby Stone back
to consciousness. She could not tell if it was opening or closing. The next sounds breaking
through the thick sedative fog were a clicking and whooshing, repeating at short intervals.

Am I on a respirator? Abby tried moving her hands. They were tied to the bed rails. She
opened her eyes. Even the subdued lighting in the room was too bright.

"Lieutenant, welcome back to the land of the living. You need to lie still. A nurse and
doctor are on their way," an accented voice said from somewhere above her.

I'm in a hospital, Abby thought, having difficulty concentrating on whoever was
talking to her.

"They will remove the breathing tube as soon as they are sure you won't need it. For
now, you need to be calm."

Although Abby could not focus her eyes, the voice was familiar, comforting. Gradually,
her vision cleared. "Keller," she tried to whisper and felt as if she were choking.

Keller was standing at the side of the bed. He was holding Abby's hand.

Abby saw a wide white bandage starting at the crown of his head and continuing down
the left side of Keller's face. "Are you okay?" She asked with her eyes.

Keller smiled.

Abby thought the faded blue hospital gown was very 'un-Marine' for him. She saw
bruises and cuts on his skin not covered fully by the gown. Eyes clearing, she saw his other
hand was holding onto a wheeled IV pole, plastic tubes snaking from his lower left arm
to a monitor. She followed the tubes. The monitor was controlling the drip rate of the
colorless fluid as it flowed from a clear plastic bag suspended at the pole's top.

Keller knew Stone's eyes were asking, *"What goes with the IV?"* He smiled. "I think they will disconnect me from Irma—that's what I call my 'girlfriend' here-- as soon as they're sure I've been shot with a truckload of antibiotics." He gazed into her eyes. "According to our Israeli docs, their biggest concern is infection." He wondered how much Abby remembered. "The shrapnel from the blast was loaded with nasty, dirty, shit." He leaned closer and whispered, "Whoever did this wanted to be sure that if we didn't die from the blast, we would die of something just as painful." He saw the shadow of fear on her face. "Don't worry. The docs insist we are all going to make a full recovery."

Abby remembered the explosion. She could almost hear the blast again.

Keller tried to smile but found it painful. "On another front, your boss is on his way here. If you did not have that tube down your throat, and couldn't talk, I'd have to caution you to say nothing about our archeological adventure." He sighed. "Not that you would say anything. You know the score."

Abby wished she knew what the score was for the bomb blast. Her mind was floating back and forth, from focusing on Keller's words to fleeting, indistinct, images of destruction and noise.

Keller continued, "While I'm on the subject, I received a message through the U.S. Embassy here in Tel Aviv. My commander in Fallujah, Major Subin, granted me a thirty-day R and R pass, to recover from my injuries. He informed me I am to assist the Israeli investigators in their inquiries. It all sounds so 'hush-hush.'"

At that moment, a doctor dressed in a crisp white lab coat over pale blue surgical scrubs opened the sliding door and entered Stone's room. He was followed by an ICU nurse, also in scrubs.

Keller, in no mood to trust anyone, looked the doctor over carefully. He guessed the doc was in his mid-fifties. Random tufts of silver hair peeked out from under a bright yellow cap. The nurse appeared to be in her late thirties. He thought her smile was friendly. He lowered his guard slightly but would observe their every move.

"Shalom, Lieutenant Stone. I am Doctor Benyoshua. This is my assistant, Mrs. Rubinov. We are going to remove the breathing tube. That will make you a lot more comfortable." He looked at Keller. "I am going to ask your friend to step out while we do this. It will only take a moment."

Keller noticed the doctor showed no trace of a Hebrew accent in his English. His accent was certainly not American. It sounded more British. "I would rather stay," he said, not wanting to leave Abby alone with someone who might hurt her. He trusted no one.

The doctor shook his head. "I understand your concern, but I assure you, Lieutenant Stone is safe with us." Leading Keller and his IV pole toward the door, as if reading Keller's mind, the doctor continued, "You are wondering about my accent. I am originally from Durban, South Africa. That is the source of my flawless English."

Keller still felt uneasy about leaving Abby unguarded. Distracted by his suspicions, he ran the IV pole over the foot of a man standing just outside Abby's room. "Excuse me. Sorry—" Civvies or no civvies, he guessed the man was an officer. Keller did his best to snap to a properly formed salute. The IV tube made that attempt futile. "Sorry, sir."

"Stand easy, Gunny. There is no saluting here," the officer in the white shirt and khaki trousers said.

"Sorry, sir," Keller repeated, noting the officer's neatly combed white hair and military bearing.

The officer leaned closer. "How did you determine I am an officer? I thought I looked pretty ordinary."

Keller replied, "It's an old habit of mine, sir. I make sure that I get to view photos of any commanding officer that has my life in his hands." He laughed. "Actually, sir, I saw your photo in the 'Big Stick's chapel office."

Breaking into a broad smile the officer said, "Good habit. I'm the Roosevelt's CO, and you must be Sergeant Keller. I'm Captain Shuster. I personally selected Rabbi Stone to serve on the Roosevelt."

"Yes, sir."

Shuster looked concerned and lowered his voice. "Tell me, Sergeant, how are you feeling? And how is Lieutenant Stone?"

"They're taking her off the respirator as we speak, sir."

"Well, that sounds like good news. I would like to visit Lt. Stone for a couple of moments."

"Absolutely sir. I understand."

The glass door slid open. Dr. Benyoshuah and Mrs. Rubinov came out, discarding their surgical gloves into a biohazard container next to the door.

Keller thought Shuster stiffened. It occurred to him that Benyoshua and Shuster may have met before.

Benhoshua directed his eyes at Shuster. "I think it's great that you came all this way to visit one of your wounded officers."

"I came all this way to make sure that what happened to Lt. Stone and Sgt. Keller doesn't happen again."

"You can go in now. Her voice is going to be a little rough. She took a pretty good hit on the head. The concussion will leave her with some significant headaches for a while. Thankfully, there is no permanent damage that we see in the CAT scan." The doctor lowered his clipboard. "I would like to keep her in a room here for at least one more day. She and the Marine were very lucky. I've been doing trauma surgery for too many bomb victims over too many years. It could have been worse...a lot worse."

Shuster nodded. "Thank you, Doctor. I appreciate your candor and discretion—"

The doctor barked a quick laugh, "There is no HIPAA in Israel. I can't get sued. HIPAA would never work here; everyone knows everyone else's business anyway—"

"Nevertheless, Doctor," Shuster began.

Benyoshua shrugged. "Okay. However, the only information that will be kept confidential is Keller and Stone's military status." He aimed his eyes at Shuster. "That is the best I can do."

Shuster did not look happy. "How long before they can return to duty?"

Casting a glance in Keller's direction, Benyoshuah replied, "Keller is strong as an ox. The scars on his back and chest testify to a significant amount of combat time. I get the impression he does not like to be away from the action too long." He shot a look at the marine. "Still, a couple of weeks off would not be a bad idea."

Shuster grunted. "His boss gave him a thirty-day pass. That should do it." He straightened. "Again, Doctor, thank you for your great care and consideration."

Benyoshua shrugged and walked away.

Captain Shuster waited until Benyoshua was gone and then turned to Keller. "You may return to your room, Sergeant. I will take it from here."

Keller wanted to stay but could not disobey an officer. He peered into Stone's room for one last look and then turned to Shuster, "I'll be in the waiting room at the end of the hall," he said, and reluctantly hobbled away.

Stone sensed someone had entered her room. "I'm not sleeping. Who's there?"

"Lieutenant Stone, it's Captain Shuster."

Stone attempted to sit up but sagged back on the pillow. "Sir, may I ask you to find the controls for this bed and raise my head?"

"No problem." Shuster raised Stone to a sitting position.

"Thank you, sir."

Shuster nodded. "Abby, how are you feeling?"

"Like shit, sir. Pardon my French."

"I have heard worse." Shuster leaned closer and lowered his voice. "Lieutenant, I have to ask, what is going on?"

"I don't understand, sir."

"You failed to report back to the ship after what was supposed to be three days of shore leave. Abby, I sent out the bloodhounds to track you down. Twelve hours later, NCIS informs me that you and this marine, Keller, and one other man, were the only survivors of a bomb attack that killed five Israelis in Tel Aviv. What the hell is going on?"

"I don't really know, sir," Stone said.

"Lieutenant, investigators from the Navy and the Israeli National Police, are chomping at the bit to interrogate you and Keller." He let this sink in. "They were 'kind' enough to inform me that this is the second attempt on your life...in a single day! So, I repeat my question. What is going on?" He pulled out a roll of antacids and popped one in his mouth. "Chaplains are supposed to solve problems, not give me heartburn." He eyed her sternly. "Are you and Keller romantically involved?"

That question, like a lightning bolt, went right to the core of her confusion. "No. Captain, sir. I am not, I repeat, not romantically involved with Sergeant Keller." How much could she tell him? "I am just helping him resolve a personal issue."

"Personal? Well, the issue must be very personal for someone. According to the police here, someone is trying to kill you."

Stone knew her naval career was on the line. With some difficulty, she swallowed and cleared her throat. She told her commanding officer as much as she thought she could about Keller's discovery of the Ezra Scroll, culminating with her two close brushes with death.

When she finished, Shuster looked frustrated. "How did you get involved in this mess in the first place?"

Stone sighed. "Keller wanted to know more about his discovery. He thought a chaplain could help. He came to me as the closest Navy rabbi." She smiled. "My bad luck."

"This is not a joking matter, Lieutenant," Shuster said. "The second man...what does this Malik character have to do with all this?"

Stone avoided eye contact with Captain Shuster. "Professor Malik was just an expert we consulted. Oh my God! I forgot all about Malik!" She heard the explosion again. "He was with us! Is he okay? Is he alive?"

Shuster placed his hand on Abby's arm. "Calm yourself. Malik is very much alive. He is in the waiting room with Sergeant Keller. He is anxious to see you. He walked away from the blast with only a few scratches." Shuster shook his head. "You were all damn lucky. Damn lucky."

"Thank God!" Stone was aware of the thin ice she was on. Shuster had already met Malik. There was no telling what the professor might have told her commanding officer. How much did Shuster already know?

Shuster straightened in his chair. "Lieutenant, according to the investigators, that bomb was meant for you and Keller." He stared at Abby. "The Israelis are very sure. In fact, they are so sure, they are, as we speak, posting a security detail outside your room and the rooms of Malik and Keller." Shuster nodded his head toward the door. Two large Israelis in street clothes, with sports jackets concealing automatic weapons, stood on either side of the entrance.

"How can they be so sure? It's not like terrorist bombs never go off in Tel Aviv—"

"One investigator put it this way: "there is only one good thing that comes out of terror bombings. The bomber blows himself up in the act.""

"I don't understand," Abby said.

"This bomber didn't blow himself up." Shuster let that sink in. "Abby, he was not a suicide bomber. He got away."

Abby mulled that over. "Are they sure?"

"That is what they said." Shuster checked his watch. "I cannot hang around to see how all of this turns out. I need to get back to our ship." He stood and looked down at Abby. "I am ordering you to be forthright with the investigators. Tell them everything you know." He gave her a paternal smile. "Since it appears your failure to report for duty, after your supposed shore leave, was not your fault, all disciplinary actions are canceled. You have a thirty-day sick leave commencing now."

"Thank you, sir."

"And Abby. Please call your mother. How she got my cell phone number, I will never know." Shuster chuckled.

"I am so sorry, sir." Abby couldn't believe it. "Thank you for the leave, sir, and your understanding."

Shuster nodded. "I expect to see you back on board the Roosevelt thirty days from now, ready and fit for duty. Is that clear?"

"Aye, aye, sir!"

Shuster turned and left the room, leaving the sliding door open. He nodded to the Israeli security detail and spoke to Keller who had returned from the waiting room, impatient to see Abby. "You can go in now, Sergeant," he said, "She's fine."

"Thank you, sir," Keller replied, wondering how much Shuster now knew. He pulled the IV pole back into Stone's room and checking that Shuster was gone whispered, "Can we talk?"

"You sound like that comedienne, Joan..."

Keller held up his free hand in a signal for Abby to be silent. He suspected the Israelis had bugged Stone's room. That was a possible explanation for why they were allowed to be together before being interrogated. Just to be sure, he held up a scrap of paper. "THE ROOM IS BUGGED," it said.

Stone nodded, wondering not for the first time, what had she gotten herself into?

CHAPTER FOUR

DATE: Tenth Day of the Fifth Month, In the Third Year Since The Destruction of Jerusalem
TIME: The Sixth Hour After Sunrise
PLACE: The Workroom of Eli the Scribe

Eli's status as one descended from a priest of a minor order did not impede his growing prominence within the inner circle of Judeans in Samaria. His acceptance in the community was a major part of Azaria's plan for Eli and their people.

Azaria revealed his hopes two weeks after Shoshana and Eli were wed. At the end of the sabbath, on a crystal-clear, starlit night, Azariah invited Eli to walk with him. "The God who protects all Israel has sent you and the sacred scrolls to us for a reason," he said.

"How can you be so sure?" Eli asked.

"Because I believe that our redemption from exile depends on what we do with the scrolls. First, we must make many copies of each scroll. Then we must teach the contents to our people, all of the people, even the Samaritans. In that way, we cannot forget who we are and where we came from."

Eli stopped walking and faced Azaria. "I am the only scribe among our people here. I cannot undertake so great a task by myself."

"Other scribes will help you."

"What other scribes?"

"The ones you train."

Soon after this talk, Azaria directed Eli to discover which members of the exile community could read and write. Eli resisted at first, feeling it was embarrassing to ask adults, far older than he, to demonstrate their abilities. It was even more embarrassing for those families who believed that their loved ones were literate to discover that they were not.

After an interval of two weeks, Azariah asked to meet Eli in the courtyard of his home. The day was cool and slightly overcast. Azariah greeted Eli while seated. He offered Eli a sweetened citrus drink and motioned for him to have a seat. "How does your survey progress? Will you find enough students for the scribal school?

Eli took a sip of his drink and shook his head slowly. "Sufficient numbers of students are not our only problem."

"What troubles you then?

Eli looked directly at Azariah. "We are drowning in languages?"

Azariah looked puzzled. "What does that mean?

Eli tried to explain. "Which language do you want our scribal school to teach?"

"What are the choices? You are the *Sofer,* you decide."

"Excellency, it's not that simple. Do we choose the language of the marketplace or the language of the Bavli rulers? Do we choose the language of Judah or the language of Samaria? Whose writing system am I supposed to teach?"

"Eli, I need to rely on your judgment. You must make the choice."

Eli sat a moment in silence, then stood up. "Our first priority must be to teach the language of the scrolls. It was the language of Abraham and Moses. It was also the language of worship in the Great House. We must ensure it is never lost or forgotten by our people."

"Eli, your instincts are filled with wisdom." Azariah smiled at him. "Our conquering rulers forced their language upon us. Daily, we speak now as they commanded. But, my son, while the Great House still stood, in the ceremonies of sacrificial worship, the sons of Levi would sing only in Hebrew. It was a bold act of defiance. Until you rescued the scrolls, our people had no hope. Teaching Hebrew now will be our daily act of defiance against the Bavlim."

Convinced of the vital importance of his mission, Eli set about his work. He first chose as teachers the priests who already had some writing skills and who could read from the sacred scrolls in Hebrew. His plan called for the creation of a school for the children of these priests. From the age of three years, these children would spend their days in school. They would start their training with alphabet and writing drills and advance to reading from the sacred scrolls themselves. What sounded initially like an easy task presented many challenges.

When Azaria visited the school, he was upset to see the precious scrolls in the hands of children. He feared they would be damaged or destroyed as they passed from tiny hand to tiny hand. "Eli," he said, "These scrolls represent the heart and soul of we Judeans in exile."

Eli replied, "These children are the heart and soul of the Judeans."

While this answer quieted Azaria, Eli realized his patron was not wrong about the need to protect the scrolls. He understood that his first responsibility was to begin the process of accurately copying each document to preserve the contents.

Understanding the demands of Eli's task, the priests provided Eli a workroom in a separate building, so he would not be disturbed by the noise in the school. A window faced the morning sun, and a makeshift scribal desk was placed next to it for light. Quills and ink were made available, along with expensive sheets of sheepskin parchment. A routine was soon established: each morning, one of the priests would bring Eli the scroll he was currently copying, along with the parchment sheets. The priest would then leave, and Eli would work for as many hours as possible before it became too dark.

Eli was determined to avoid mistakes, so he forced himself to work slowly, carefully forming each letter in the style that his beloved teacher, Akkub, son of Shallum, had taught him. He soon realized he could only work during the time that light flooded into his window. If he worked in the presence of oil lamps, the parchment would become stained with soot.

As he began his transcriptions, Eli discovered that each parchment sheet could bear forty lines of text in six columns, each being about a handbreadth in width. He estimated at his current pace, he could only manage about one sheet per month. He became painfully aware that the whole process was taking too long. He needed help but none was available.

When the light became too poor for Eli to work, he would walk the short dirt path to the school and observe the students and the teachers at their lessons. Those who worked well with a stylus in sand or dirt, he advanced to quill and ink on sheepskin. At each level, he watched the students for any hint of artistic talent. He was on the lookout for students who might serve as apprentice scribes. There was no time to lose. He felt he was in a desperate race to duplicate and preserve the scrolls. There was no telling when something might happen to endanger their lives and cause the loss of the precious texts. He swore that he would not let that happen.

CHAPTER FIVE

DATE: March 17, 2009
TIME: 1:30 P. M. Local Time
PLACE: Step Down Unit, Souraski Medical Center, Tel Aviv

Keller, aware that listening devices were probably concealed in Stone's hospital room, focused on small talk. It was not easy. He tried to get Stone to talk about football games in Ann Arbor. And she, quickly getting the idea, tried to get Keller to talk about growing up in Charleston. Neither effort was successful. What they wanted to talk about was the bombing and who was out to get them.

The Israeli security officers stationed at the room door should have made Keller feel Abby was safe, but he wondered if they were also eavesdropping on their conversation. As the minutes passed, Keller became increasingly frustrated and impatient.

Rising on her elbow, Stone muttered, "I need to get out of here. Get my clothes, please?"

Keller looked at Abby. "I don't think I will be allowed to do that, Lieutenant."

A voice came from the doorway. "The Sergeant is absolutely correct, Lt Stone. For the time being, both of you are going nowhere. I am Lt. Col. Natan Lavi. I am with the Police." The speaker was tall with an athletic build, wearing the crisply pressed uniform of a senior officer in the Israeli Police. His English carried the trace of a Hebrew accent. He entered and stood at the foot of the bed.

Keller noticed that the security officers did not challenge Lavi's entry. He was known to them.

Stone's eyes shot at the visitor. "I do not take orders from the Israeli Police!"

Lavi smiled. "Because you have been involved in a terrorist incident with significant loss of life, you have become a person of interest in our investigation. You will take orders from me. Shall I call Captain Shuster and let you explain your concerns to him?"

Stone lay back in her bed, glowering at Lavi. "So, now that you are in charge, what comes next?"

Lavi replied, "Your doctor has released you from the ICU and you have been assigned to a Step-Down unit on the Second Floor. In a few moments, you and your bed will be transferred to a VIP private room. In the meantime, one of my officers will assist Sergeant Keller as he completes the paperwork discharging him as a patient." He glanced at Keller. "Sergeant Keller will join us in your new room after that is accomplished."

Keller grimaced. "I'm being assigned a babysitter to make sure I don't disappear?"

"Those are your words, Sergeant, not mine," said Lavi and continued calmly. "After Lt. Stone is settled in her new room, and you both have a chance to have some lunch, we will commence our interview. If there are no questions, I will see you after lunch."

Keller watched Lavi leave the room and glanced at Stone. "We're persons of interest," he said.

Abby nodded.

Keller escorted Abby as she was moved to her new room. Once settled, lunch was brought in for them by two Israeli police officers.

"They're not taking any chances," Keller said to Abby, pulling the cover off his entrée. He was surprised that he enjoyed his hospital lunch, 'two cuts above Marine Meals-Ready-to-Eat.'

As they ate in silence, Keller surveyed the room, still wondering if it was bugged. He thought the VIP room was cheery, sunny, and large for a hospital. He noted a semicircle of six folding chairs had been placed around the foot of Lt. Stone's bed. At present, only Keller and Stone were in the room, so he suspected the chairs had been arranged for a group interrogation. A new pair of security officers were stationed at the room's entrance.

Abby also wondered if the room was bugged.

Keller finished his meal and took a seat at the left edge of the semi-circle, close to Abby's bed. He watched silently as she poked at chicken schnitzel, rice, and asparagus. He waited impatiently until Stone finished picking at the meal. "You ready for this interview, Lieutenant?" he asked, as she took a sip of orange juice.

Stone shook her head. "Might as well get this over with. Send in the clowns."

Keller was surprised. "You don't mean that, do you?"

Stone closed her eyes. "I'm frustrated and very tired. Let's get this over with."

Keller shuffled to the door. "We're ready for you, now." He was surprised to see a familiar face. It was Sergeant Ramon, the police officer who rescued them on the Jerusalem-Tel Aviv Highway. She was followed by Lt. Col. Lavi and two others.

Lavi introduced the two newcomers. "Lt. Stone and Sergeant Keller, allow me to introduce my colleagues from the *Shirutei Bitachon*, the Security Service, what you might know as the Shin Bet. This is Omar, and this is Rafi, his boss. The Shin Bet is sort of a combination FBI and CIA."

Keller appraised the superior officer, Rafi, a mildly-handsome, fortyish Israeli. He was just under six feet tall, with the upper body of someone who worked out regularly. He wore a white short-sleeved, open-collar shirt, with epaulets on the shoulders. Khaki work pants and sandals without socks completed his "regular-guy' Israeli look.

Keller then turned his eyes to the other Shin Bet official. Omar appeared to be in his late thirties, no more than five-feet-eight- inches tall, and slight of build. He wore a faded navy-blue polo shirt with olive green cargo pants. What attracted Keller's eyes was the bulge on Omar's right hip, about the size of a nine-millimeter Baretta, or whatever the Israelis used as the semi-automatic pistol of choice. He studied Omar's face, marked with deep craters on his cheeks, and was uncertain if the blemishes were from a skin disease, grafts over a bad burn, or both. Overall, the effect was a bit menacing, helpful during an interrogation, he thought, as he returned to Abby's side.

Both Shin Bet officers took seats in the semi-circle.

Keller eyed Abby. He hoped the questioning would not hurt her recovery.

Ramon and Lavi took turns as the interview began. Their initial questions sought details of the crash on the highway. They appeared intent on learning what Keller and Stone could supply to help identify the driver of the dump truck that crashed into them, nearly sending them off the embankment.

Abby was confused. "Why are you going back to that accident?" She asked, closing her eyes.

Keller saw Abby was upset and wanted to help. "Wait a minute. Do you guys think the truck driver and the bomber are the same individual?" He caught a quick exchange of eye contact between the two Shin Bet officers and the policemen.

Keller smiled. "I'm right, aren't I? Come on, I got it, didn't I?"

"Nothing gets by you, Sergeant, does it?" Lt. Col. Lavi responded. "Actually, there is no way we can confirm that, as of now. The best we can say is that we believe the two attacks may be connected."

"Connected? By what?" Keller demanded, seeing Abby's eyes were still closed.

The senior Shin Bet officer took the lead. "It is probable the attacks came from the same source. An eyewitness came forward with a description of the presumed bomber. It may link up with the truck driver."

Ramon spoke in a more sympathetic tone. Her accent was more pronounced than Lavi's. "Both men were wearing shirts with an unusual red crown logo—"

Stone opened her eyes. "You know who these guys are, don't you," she said, staring at Lavi.

Lavi glanced at Ramon and gave a subtle nod.

Ramon said softly, "What we can tell you so far, is that this group is not, strictly speaking, a terrorist organization—"

"What? Really?" Keller was through with splitting hairs. "We know it was a bomb, and they definitely tried to push us off a cliff. I don't understand how you can say they're not terrorists—"

Ramon replied, "Sergeant, if we are correct, this organization has never committed a violent act against anyone. They do not consider Israel, or the Israeli government, to be their enemy. We have no record of weapons trading or acquisitions on their part—"

Lavi interrupted. "Not one of their members or leaders has ever been arrested for anything more serious than trespassing." He aimed his eyes at Stone. "Since the end of the Six Day War in June 1967, they have been an advocacy group for civil rights and recognition as a religious group under the Basic Laws of the State of Israel." He shook his head. "From all that we know about this community, these two violent acts make no sense. No sense at all."

"So, who are these paragons of virtue?" Keller asked, not understanding any of this.

Lavi glanced at a manila file in his hand. "They call themselves *Keter Shomron.*"

Stone looked up. "The Crown of Samaria? Oh my God! They're Samaritans!"

CHAPTER SIX

DATE: Fourth Day of the Fourth Month In the Tenth Year Since the Destruction of Jerusalem
TIME: Just Before Sunset
PLACE: The Scribal School of the Judeans on the Edge of Pumbedita, in the Kingdom of Babylonia

After opening the door to the parchment storeroom, Zadok stood motionless, tears streaming down his face. Even after ten long years, the look and smell of old parchment scrolls triggered intense feelings of loneliness and loss. The scrolls were painful reminders of the absence of his beloved twin brother, Eli.

Zadok and Eli, his brother, had been apprentice scribes perfecting their skills when their lives were upended by war. Bavli armies had mounted an unrelenting siege to the mount of the Sacred House. During the twins' harrowing escape from Jerusalem, in flames, the brothers rescued the precious scrolls from the scribal school in the Sacred House. They were determined to pursue the caravan of Judean exiles in their march from Jerusalem and present the scrolls to the leaders of their people.

Ezekiel ben Buzi was the highest-ranking priest in the camp of the exiles. He understood the value of the scrolls and was convinced that to ensure their survival, it would be necessary to divide the scrolls, keeping half with the exiles and sending the others, for safety, to Samaria. Eli was assigned the mission of taking the scrolls intended for Samaria while his brother was sent with the exiles. That was the last time Zadok had been with his brother. Was Eli still alive?

Zadok entered the storeroom to search for an exercise scroll that would help one of his students. The light was weak at this time of day. As he rolled and unrolled the scrolls, he suddenly stopped. "What is this doing here?" he asked, examining a scroll that he did not recognize. The calligraphy was good, but clearly not of the highest master scribe quality.

Holding the document up to the light, he noted the parchment was not bleached. It was darker than the other scrolls, which made reading from it more difficult. This is not a product of this school, he thought. It might have been written before the destruction of Judah. As he examined it further, he became certain it was not one of the scrolls he and Eli saved from the burning Sacred House.

Over the ten years he had been in Bavel, Zadok had memorized everything about the scrolls: their size, weight, color, thickness, length, calligraphy style, and content. He learned to appreciate that each Judean scroll rescued from the Sacred House told a story. Most of the stories he knew from childhood. His relatives told the twins stories of the Sons of Israel as evening entertainment. Each uncle and older cousin enthusiastically embellished the stories to hold the attention of their young listeners. He loved listening to these exciting tales which he then believed to be the true history of his people. When during the first month of his journey in exile he found time to read, he was disappointed. The scroll version was not as exciting as the storyteller's adventures he remembered. He understood that his relatives and the generations of those who handed down the oral versions had added their own personal touches to what was contained in the written texts.

Now, as he read this unfamiliar scroll, he realized he had never heard this narrative before. He leaned over the scroll, fascinated at reading how the Eternal God of Israel instructed Moses to build him a dwelling, a *mishkan*. Even as the light grew dim, Zadok's excitement increased as the scroll recounted how this house of God was to be a moveable shelter that would follow the Israelites wherever they went. He learned how artisans were to build this sacred 'tent' adhering to detailed descriptions presented by the Eternal to Moses, and when the *mishkan*, was completed, the Eternal God would come to reside within this dwelling. It would be the site of contact between the Eternal and Moses.

"This is amazing," Zadok thought as he read God's instructions for daily sacrifices and festival offerings that would take place within the enclosed space. He marveled at the details, as even sacred objects of bronze and gold, dedicated to the operation of the *mishkan*, were painstakingly described by the author of this hitherto unknown scroll. Straining to read the last words in the disappearing twilight, Zadok was moved almost to tears by the writer's descriptions of the huge structure. It brought back his childhood memories of the Sacred House in Jerusalem. His memories may have been distorted by the passage of time, but he realized the *mishkan* enclosure described was nearly as large as the area of the inner court of the Sacred House built by Solomon, the son of David. His heart raced. This scroll was a revelation he could not keep to himself. He had to show it at once to his patron and mentor, Ezekiel, the lead priest of the Judeans in exile.

Ezekiel lived well for a Judean exile. His house, though not large for an important person, was uphill and upwind, so when it rained, water flowed away from its foundation, and when the stench of rotting garbage wafted through the exiles' neighborhood, it was swept away from his home. The wall that faced west had no windows so dust would not blow directly into the house from the desert. A small garden flanked the front entrance on the east side.

When Zadok ran through the gateless opening in the low mud-brick wall, Ezekiel was bent over pulling up weeds from the garden. "Mar Ezekiel! Mar Ezekiel," he shouted, "I have discovered...there is another scroll—"

Ezekiel stood. "Zadok, take hold of yourself. Calm down." He shook his head at the younger man's lack of decorum. "What are you going on about? Another scroll?"

Zadok could barely catch his breath. "In the storeroom...at the school... it is very old. I cannot understand why it was not noticed before... it must have been stuck between other scrolls—"

Ezekiel smiled. "You must calm yourself. Now, when did you find this so-called new scroll?"

Zadok took several deep breaths. "I found it as the sun was just descending below the Temple of Marduk. I never saw it before."

Ezekiel nodded patiently. "Do you have the scroll with you?"

"Of course, my teacher, I would not let it out of my sight." Zadok reached inside of his tunic and drew out the end of the scroll.

Ezekiel shook his head. "The light is dim. Let's go inside and take a good look." As he entered his house, he lit oil lamps along the way. He led Zadok into a room furnished with a table and two stools. The priest lit two more lamps and placed them on the table. He then motioned for Zadok to hand him the scroll. He carefully unrolled the parchment and stretched it across the table. "It looks to be very old. It is brittle." He leaned over the scroll. "Now, let's see what you have found."

Zadok stood motionless, for what seemed like an eternity as Ezekiel unrolled the scroll slowly, from end to end. Ezekiel began reading the lines silently, but soon was reading out loud.

Zadok hung onto every word. He became impatient when his teacher read the scroll a second time. Then a third. Zadok was puzzled but did not interrupt. Was this a genuine discovery or something else? Ezekiel would know.

It was nearly the middle of the night when Ezekiel looked up at Zadok and said softly, "This is what our people need. It is a clear sign from the Eternal One, delivered by your hand." He stared into Zadok's eyes. "You just may have begun the redemption of Judah."

"How is that possible? It's a good story at best, but still, just a story." Zadok was surprised that his discovery might be of such significance.

"Zadok, our people are dying here in exile. They lack hope and they lack faith in our eventual return to Judah. Not a day goes by when some old Judean family abandons the God of Abraham and Jacob and make sacrifices to Tammuz, Ishtar or Marduk. Our people are forgetting who they are and what the Eternal One promised us." Ezekiel sighed deeply. "Even some of our priests, those who once served on the priestly watches in the Sacred House in Jerusalem, are giving up hope and turning to false gods."

"But surely, you do not mean that our priests have become idol worshippers?"

"Not all, but some of the younger ones have. The remaining faithful priests still gather in my home. We talk of return and renewal." Ezekiel looked sympathetically at Zadok. "We read a few lines from the rescued scrolls, tell a few stories of Judah and Jerusalem, heave deep and mournful sighs, and then return to the business of daily survival as exiles. We few have not lost our hope and faith." He shook his head sadly. "But most of our people do nothing and have lost their faith. When your generation dies, I am afraid there will be no one left who remembers our land and sacred city." He fell silent and closed his eyes.

Zadok suspected Ezekiel was seeking guidance from the Eternal God. He had witnessed Ezekiel fall into this trance-like state many times. After a few moments, the priest would speak, but not to anyone nearby. It was as if his patron was speaking to God. After the first time Zadok witnessed Ezekiel in this strange state, he decided to record the priest's words. Much was babble rather than coherent language, but Zadok did the best he could at retaining every syllable.

When the trance ended and Ezekiel opened his eyes, Zadok would read the words back to Ezekiel and the priest would explain and elaborate on their meaning. All of which Zadok would capture on parchment.

Now, Zadok grabbed a fresh sheet, quill, and a jar of ink from a wooden shelf. He retook his seat opposite the priest. In fits and starts, he wrote almost to the breaking of dawn, when Ezekiel shouted, "You know, my God. You know, my God," and fell asleep. Only then did Zadok stop writing, and his head dropped to the table.

An hour after dawn, a braying ass, responding to the lash of its master, awakened them. Ezekiel's eyes opened, bright and clear as if he had a night of untroubled sleep. Zadok, on the other hand, was exhausted, eyes clouded, barely able to see.

"Come, Zadok. Let's get some breakfast in the market," Ezekiel said.

Zadok yawned. "Are we not going to talk of what happened in the night?"

"What do you mean, what happened in the night?" Ezekiel laughed at Zadok's concerned face. "Rest easy! I am teasing you. Of course, we will talk. We have much work to do. But first, we must have food to give us strength." He dropped his hand on Zadok's shoulder. "I now know what our God intends for us."

"Does it have something to do with the scroll?"

"It has everything to do with the scroll. But you must be patient. I need some olives, cheese, and bread."

"The Eternal speaks to you and your first thought is food?"

"When the people hunger, they cannot hear the word of the Eternal."

"Did the Eternal tell you that?"

"No, I am telling you that. Go wash your face. It will wake you up."

There were only a few stalls open in the market of Pumbedita. It was not a market day, so farmers were not bringing food. Nevertheless, Ezekiel was able to locate what he sought and added a clay flask of *sikaru*, a drink made from dates and honey. He then led Zadok back to a nearby clearing, where he sat on the ground beneath a tree, where they enjoyed their breakfast under its abundant shade.

Even as he enjoyed his meal, Zadok was impatient to know what his discovery had unleashed in the priest.

Finally, Ezekiel downed his drink and said, "The Eternal has announced to me His intention to restore our people." He tossed the leftover scraps of their breakfast to a mangy tan and white dog that followed them from the market.

Zadok was disappointed. "But you have already had many such visions of our return before this—"

"Yes, my son, but this vision was different. It was not about the return of only Judah." He raised his hands. "The Eternal spoke to me about the whole house of Israel." He smiled benevolently at Zadok. "The God of Israel promised to reunite all of the sons of Israel, including those who have disappeared—"

Zadok interrupted. "You know as well as I, they have not disappeared. Their great-grandchildren walk among us. The Assyrians were determined to beat God out of the tribe of Ephraim."

"Zadok, you are right, the Assyrians were successful. Not one of that tribe attends our schools or meetings. They will have nothing to do with us or our God. But the Bavlim are different."

"One conqueror is like another."

"Not so, my young scribe. The Bavlim tolerate the gods of their subjects. It has helped them rule over a thousand distinct peoples. They understand that if you allow a people their gods, they will remain calm, not rebel. Take their gods from them and they will hate you forever." He nodded his head thoughtfully. "The Bavlim are masters at ruling an empire because they understand that tolerating their subjects' gods eliminates a great source of rebellion. We, my friend, are going to make great use of that crucial difference between Ashur and Bavel. I believe The Eternal intends for Judah to give the entire house of Israel hope, through us."

"And how is that supposed to happen?"

Ezekiel smiled. "We are going to build a *mishkan* for the Eternal, here, in Bavel. Our people will be reborn, resurrected from the living death of exile. The building of this sanctuary will be the beginning of our return as a unified people."

"Now you sound like a Persian priest, with your talk of resurrection—"

"I only use this phrase as a way of describing our situation. But, as your notes testify, that is what the Eternal revealed to me. The dry bones of Israel in exile will be resurrected to renewed life in Zion."

Zadok sighed. "I do not understand how building this *mishkan* can resurrect our people."

Ezekiel was patient with his pupil. "First, it will bring them together for a common purpose, the building of a house for God. Second, it will provide an opportunity to teach our people about the sacred scrolls. They will learn their content. They will come to understand, to believe, that there will be an end to our exile. Third, it will provide us with a place to serve the Eternal, to worship our God, in the midst of the Bavlim, so our faith will not die as it is doing now."

"And how do you think the Bavlim will respond to your plan, assuming we can get our people to unite for this goal?"

Ezekiel stared gently into Zadok's eyes. "Zadok, it is not my plan. It is the plan of the Eternal. But to answer your question, the Bavlim have prohibited us from building a sacred house. But we are not building a permanent structure. We will build a *mishkan*, a moveable sanctuary—"

"And you think the Bavlim will understand the difference?"

"The Bavlim will accept this devotion to our God, so long as our people follow their laws and make no attempt at rebellion. That is what separates them from the Assyrians."

Ezekiel brushed crumbs from his tunic, stretched, and let out a yawn, then rose to his feet and started walking. "Zadok, son of Achituv, we have work to do. We need to present the *Mishkan Scroll* to the next gathering of the council of the elders of Judah."

"But they will not gather until the rains fall in the ninth month."

Ezekiel turned back to Zadok. "Then we will have ample time to prepare copies of the *Mishkan Scroll* so that they can read it for themselves."

Zadok hurried after his master, wondering if his discovery would unleash new hope for his people or a new and grave threat to their existence.

CHAPTER SEVEN

DATE: March 17, 2009
TIME: 2:30 P. M. Local Time
PLACE: Step Down Unit, Souraski Medical Center, Tel Aviv

Keller shook his head in disbelief. "You have got to be kidding. Samaritans? Really? Samaritans actually exist?"

Lavi shifted uncomfortably, in his chair. "They really do exist."

Keller only knew of one kind of Samaritan, a 'good Samaritan,' someone who saves a life. What did these murderous Samaritan assassins have to do with his scroll? He was determined to find out. "In the States, we build Good Samaritan Hospitals. People are recognized with awards that bear that name. Now you say you believe real live Samaritans are trying to kill tourists, forcing them off the Jerusalem highway and throwing bombs?" He shook his head. "I don't get it."

"We don't understand it either," said Lavi.

Stone sat up and looked at Keller. "Sergeant, everything in this part of the world is touched by history. Two thousand years ago, most ancient Judeans despised the Samaritans. The feeling was mutual."

Keller looked perplexed. "This two-thousand-year-old grudge is why we're being attacked? Whatever happened to the Good Samaritan?"

Stone reached for a hospital robe draped across her bed. Still aching from her injuries, she slid off the edge of the mattress and wrapped the robe around her. "The story of the "Good Samaritan" is told by Jesus in the New Testament. His point is memorable because the Samaritan, who is expected to hate Judeans, provides life-saving assistance to a severely wounded Judean, who had been left to die in the middle of a road by his own people."

Sergeant Ramon. looking out the window at the Tel Aviv skyline, turned to face Keller. "It is not a bad lesson for all to learn. How we judge people should be based on their actions, not their race, religion, or politics. Perhaps, Rabbi Stone, you should incorporate this story into your next sermon. But can we get back to the central problem? If we assume our unknown killer, or killers, are Samaritans, why are they targeting you? They want you very dead, very badly." She pointed her finger at Keller. "What have you done to piss these people off? It must be something big. We have never had a problem with any of them before."

Lavi stood and made his way to the door. He opened it a few inches and motioned one of the security officers to approach. "Please bring Professor Malik here, now. It's time we heard from him."

Keller was surprised when, in less than a moment, a soft knock on the door indicated Malik had arrived. How did the professor get here so fast, he wondered.

Malik entered the room still in blue scrubs, but no longer connected to an IV pole. Though the others were seated, he remained standing, his back to the window.

Lavi cleared his throat and addressed the room. "I suppose it's time to re-introduce you all to Dr. Shlomo Malik. Our American guests know him as Professor Malik of Tel Aviv University. We know him better as Colonel Shlomo Malik of the MOSSAD."

Keller and Stone exchanged wide-eyed looks of surprise.

"Holy shit! Did you know about this?" Keller whispered.

"It's the first I heard," Stone replied.

Malik smiled sheepishly. "Sorry, *Chaverim*. I am not supposed to reveal my status unless it helps in getting our work done."

Lavi faced Malik. "You were able to overhear our entire interview so far. Any thoughts?"

Malik nodded his head slowly. "This is all about the scroll Keller discovered. I'm convinced whoever tried to kill us was trying to stop us from learning its contents."

Ramon turned toward Malik, "Why would anyone wish to prevent you from deciphering a scroll that, until a few days ago, did not exist?"

Malik paced the floor. "As far as **you** are concerned, Sergeant Ramon, the scroll did not exist. But my family has always known it must exist. Hell, if you were, like me, a Jew growing up in Fallujah, you would have heard stories about the Ezra Scroll, on a nearly daily basis."

Keller shook his head in disbelief. "I heard stories of Santa Claus in Charleston all my life. Just because you hear daily stories about something, doesn't mean it's real."

Ramon shared Keller's skepticism. "There are Jews in Fallujah?"

Malik stopped pacing, looking at Ramon. "There were hundreds of Jews there before 1960. Back then, was an exceedingly dangerous time. Iraqi Jewish leaders made sure the community gave no offense to the government. Jews living in Iraq were struggling for survival. The legend of the Ezra Scroll allowed Jews in Iraq to feel pride as Jews. Many fervently believed that if the Ezra Scroll were ever discovered, it would lead to an original copy of the Torah, the Five Books of Moses."

"That still does not answer our central question," Ramon said.

Rafi, the senior Shin Bet officer, aimed his eyes at Malik. "There must be something in that scroll the Samaritans do not want revealed."

Omar, his colleague, spoke up for the first time. "We do not have any idea what the *Shomronim*, Samaritans, may be trying to hide. The truth is, they have been, until now, practically invisible. To our government, they are an anachronism, a surviving remnant of a people long forgotten by history and treated by Christians and Muslims alike, as harmless, powerless, heretics."

Stone laughed. "Powerless heretics with bombs and ten-ton dump trucks."

Omar didn't miss a beat. "In 1948, the surviving Samaritan community, numbering some 200 souls, was centered in and around Nablus on the West Bank, currently a part of the Palestinian Authority. The rest of the Samaritans lived in Israel, around the city of Holon."

Keller shot an exasperated look at Stone. She appeared to be absorbed in what he considered a history lesson.

Omar continued, "After the 1967 war, came our occupation of the West Bank, including Nablus. The Samaritans there, and in Israel, were treated as very special communities. Despite the real political tensions between Israelis and Palestinians, arguing over every detail in the peace process, the two Samaritan communities were now able to travel freely back and forth across lines that still divided Arabs from Jews."

"They could travel wherever they wanted?" Stone asked.

Omar nodded. "The Samaritan's unique Biblical identity saved them from the constant scrutiny our security services directed toward Palestinian Arabs."

"Where is all of this going?" Keller asked.

Rafi held his hand out in a calming gesture. "*Savlanut*, patience, Sergeant."

Omar continued. "There was a problem. Young Samaritans did not like being 'exhibits in a Biblical Zoo.' They wanted to determine their own fate, not have it forced upon them, not by their ultra-conservative parents, not by the Israelis, and not by the Palestinians. A narrow window of freedom opened when West Bank Samaritans were given unfettered access to Israel."

"How do you know all this stuff? Are you a Samaritan?" Keller asked.

Rafi explained. "Omar is a member of the Israeli Druse community. He is a cultural anthropologist who holds a PhD from your Michigan State University. He wrote his dissertation on the Samaritans."

Stone smirked. "Michigan State, in East Lansing, is not exactly a hotbed of Near Eastern Studies."

Omar looked Stone in the eyes. "I know this is hard for a Wolverine to accept, but there are some things that are better at Michigan State than at the University of Michigan."

Stone was not prepared for a Druse stranger to make smart-ass remarks about her ties to Ann Arbor. The realization hit that the *Shin Bet* officer had studied her jacket.

Keller pointed an accusing finger at Omar. "Stop playing games with us. You knew the attacks were coming from someone connected with Samaritans. It's more than a coincidence that you just happened to accompany Rafi to this meeting. You just happen to be an expert on a people, who, according to your fable, do not matter in the larger scheme of things." He shook his head. "I really respect you guys and your reputation for toughness, tenacity, and preparation. So, cut the bullshit. What's going on? Really."

"As you wish, Sergeant Keller," said Rafi. "I shall have to rely on your discretion. Nothing we say here gets out of this room. Omar, fill them in on our ancient 'friends' recent activities."

Omar nodded. "We started paying closer attention to the *Shomronim*, the Samaritans, as you say, just after Hamas took control of Gaza."

"Shall I call you Agent Omar or Professor Omar?" Stone said.

"Omar is just fine."

"What's Hamas got to do with Samaritans? Their strength has always been in Gaza." Stone asked.

Omar nodded in agreement. "You are correct, but Hamas wants it all. They want to rule Gaza and the rest of Palestine for starters, on their way to destroying Israel and claiming all of it for an Islamic republic.

Rafi cleared his throat. "A year ago, our communications surveillance of Hamas revealed that their operatives approached a few young Samaritans living in Nablus. Playing on their sense of powerlessness, Hamas offered them a deal. If the Samaritans would support Hamas in its efforts to throw the PA out of the West Bank, then Hamas would guarantee the well-being of the Samaritan community. The guarantee included designating tracts of land close to the sight of their ancient temple on Mt. Gerizim, as Samaritan property; funding to build a new temple there; and land for housing and growing the community. Hamas even made a one-time offer to resettle the Samaritans living in Israel, back on the West Bank, at Hamas's expense.

Omar took over. "My research on the Samaritan community allowed me to interview their leadership. Most Samaritans on the West Bank believe that a Palestinian State has no room for them. The Palestinian Authority, currently in control of the West Bank, has always treated the Samaritans as spies for Israel. The Samaritans expect the radicals in the PA to force their expulsion and confiscate what little property they still have. The young Samaritan radicals felt they had nothing left to lose. And so, they formed *Keter Shomron,* the Crown of Samaria, to do Hamas bidding."

Malik paused his pacing. "What possible help could *Keter Shomron* provide Hamas?"

"There are two ways these young Samaritans can assist Hamas," Rafi said. "First, Samaritans have almost unfettered access to both Israel and the West Bank. This gives them the potential to smuggle weapons parts, cell phones, electronic devices, and messages for Hamas. Because we were blinded by their historic impotence, we never paid them any attention."

"And the second way?" Keller asked.

Rafi removed his glasses and started to clean them. "Perceptions matter a great deal in the Middle East. They are often more important than truth. The second way the Samaritans could give aid and comfort to Hamas is to disrupt and challenge the Zionist version of history. Hamas has made serious efforts to de-legitimize Jewish claims to *Eretz Yisrael*. They enjoy playing with Western European guilt over the *Shoah*. In their propaganda, the Jews of Israel are no better than Nazis. Even mainstream Islam routinely asserts that the Jews distorted the text of the Bible. Hamas has never missed an opportunity to raise questions as to the accuracy of Biblical history, especially divine promises to Jews. For Hamas, the bottom line is, that the Jews who settled here in the 19th and 20th centuries are imposters and are not the descendants of David and Solomon. Every doubt planted in the minds of ordinary Europeans makes it easier to challenge Israel's political and economic status with the European Union."

Omar jumped in. "The Samaritans are perfect foils for Hamas. They have always claimed that they are not Jews, that they were the true Israel. This means only they are entitled to the land of Israel because God put them on the land which the northern Kingdom of Israel forfeited through its disobedience and idolatry."

Rafi added, "The Samaritans see themselves as the ever-faithful keepers of God's commandments. Whatever is contained in the Ezra Scroll, or whatever it may lead to, might be strong enough proof to deny the historical claims of the Samaritans and render them useless to Hamas."

"What a load of camel shit!"

All eyes turned toward Malik.

"What group of terrorist idiots wear logo imprinted t-shirts announcing their identity to surviving witnesses?" Malik asked.

Rafi asked, "Do you have an answer, Colonel?"

Malik nodded slowly. "We are all missing something. I believe there is another player in this dangerous game."

Keller wondered who he meant.

CHAPTER EIGHT

DATE: Tenth Day of the Ninth Month, in the Tenth Year, since the Destruction of Jerusalem
TIME: First Hour of the Third Watch
PLACE: The Judean Settlement on the Edge of Pumbedita In the Kingdom of Babylonia

Winter rains arrived early in lower Bavel. Grey skies made everything appear drab and colorless, except for the yellow mud that overran all the pathways. The river *Frat (Euphrates)* was running fast and high. During this season, houses made with mud brick and thatched roofs required constant repairs to prevent collapse. Zadok's house was no exception. This was the reason he was on the top of a crudely made ladder placed against his house. After going at this task for two hours in intermittent rain, he started throwing palm fronds randomly on the roof, hoping for the best.

Miryam, his wife, was passing fronds up to him. "Take your time, Zadok. You will leave holes and your sons will get wet. We cannot allow them to get sick with fever again. A dry house is a healthy house."

"What Bavli thatcher told you that one?"

Miryam passed up another frond. "Maybe you should leave this work for a Bavli thatcher. They actually know what they're doing,"

Zadok leaned down and took a frond from Miryam and dropped it into an open space on the roof. "You know as well as I do that we cannot afford to have a Bavli do the job. It's just that my heart and mind are not in this work. As I speak with you, the council of elders of Judah is gathering in Mar Ezekiel's home. I need to be there!"

"The council will have to wait. This roof is more important."

Zadok knew Miryam was right. She was wise and remarkably stubborn.

Miryam was the eldest daughter of Yonatan, the silversmith. Zadok had met Yonatan, at one of the regular Sabbath meetings of Judean exiles in the house of Ezekiel ben Buzi. In their initial conversation, they discovered that both of their families were originally from Gezer in Judah. Yonatan admired Zadok's skills as a scribe and teacher. He believed the young man would make someone a good husband; why not for his eldest daughter, Miryam?

In the four years since their wedding in Ezekiel's garden, Zadok and Miryam grew in their love for one another. Each had a sense of humor while enduring the hardships of exile. Each was an optimist in the face of the harsh realities of survival. Daily, Zadok expressed gratitude to the God of their ancestors that Miryam gave birth to two healthy sons. He also gave thanks that Miryam was beautiful and modest, caring and kind. Despite living the hard life of a Judean exile, Zadok knew he was blessed.

One day in late spring, as their second son approached the day marking his first year, Miryam decided she wanted more out of her life. She was determined to get Zadok to see things from her point of view. She paid a surprise visit to Zadok's workroom.

Zadok looked up from the scroll he was cleaning. "Miryam, where are the boys? Are they sick?"

"The boys are with my parents. They're fine. Here, these can be made into pens for your students." She placed a small basket filled with goose feathers on the table. Then, she suddenly grasped Zadok by his shoulders and looked him in the eye. "Teach me to read and write, my husband?"

With his brows raised in surprise, Zadok asked, "What brought this on?"

"My life is so narrow, so closed in. There are times when I have done the cooking, and the cleaning, and the boys are napping when I just sit and stare at the walls of our home. I could be doing something worthwhile. I can be helping you."

"You are helping me. You are doing something worthwhile."

Shaking her head, Miryam said, "Plucking goose feathers for your pens is not enough. Cleaning ink jars is not enough. I know, that when you are reading, you are in another place, another world. I want to experience that, not through some storyteller, but on my own."

Zadok could not say no to her. He loved her too much. Realizing how intensely important this was to Miryam, and not wanting to disappoint her, Zadok agreed to teach her. Those lessons almost ended their marriage.

Zadok, the master scribe, was not used to being interrupted by his students. He taught. They listened. When Zadok sought to instruct Miryam, he taught. She asked questions. She wanted to know every rule of grammar and spelling. She wanted to know the reason for everything. She accepted nothing on faith. Her desire to learn to read and write was also fed by her resentment of the way Judean tradition treated women, binding them to housework and childrearing.

Though they sometimes battled mightily, Miryam turned out to be a very adept pupil. In a single year, she exceeded the level of knowledge of Zadok's best third-year students. She could prepare skins for parchment despite the considerable strength it took to stretch them on frames. She mastered the art of brewing ink, trimming feathers into quills, and shaping points on the end of the quills. Most of all, she had an artist's eye toward forming letters. She did not simply write letters; she drew them with great care. She was making herself into a true *soferet*, a scribe. Her reading skills were equal to her scribal skills. After working with Zadok, in her spare time she had read all of the scrolls preserved from the Sacred House and even copied sections for practice. Today, as she watched Zadok working on the roof, Miryam worried that her husband might fall.

The rain, which began as a drizzle increased in intensity, soaking Zadok through to his skin. "Hold the ladder steady. I'm coming down. Where are the boys?"

Miryam shouted, "Do you want me to hold the ladder or find the boys?"

"You know what I mean."

Miryam handed Zadok a large dry cloth. "They are at my father's work bench watching him melt silver or copper, or whatever. It's always something with fire. He makes them think that he is a magician, and they love it."

"I only hope that your father has enough sense to keep the boys from hurting themselves with fire."

"Zadok, my father loves those boys almost as much as you do. Besides, being in his shed is not a bad thing on a cold and damp day." Miryam cleared her throat. "Zadok, there is something I must speak with you about."

"Of course. What is it?"

Before Miryam could reveal her news, Yeshuah ben Yozadak, a priest and Ezekiel's assistant, came riding up on a grey and black ass. Yeshuah was a heavy load even for this beast of burden.

Zadok thought there is nothing noble or elegant about a person sitting astride an ass. In most cases, the legs and feet of the rider were longer than the ass was tall. This was indeed the case with Yeshuah. His feet were dragging on the ground, making it appear as if he were helping the ass to walk.

Yeshuah tightened his grip on the reins of the ass. "My lord scribe, I bring you a message from Ezekiel the High Priest."

Eyes wide with surprise, Zadok did not respond. He refused to acknowledge this priest's florid and undeserved terms of address. He was just a scribe. Ezekiel was just a priest, nothing more.

Clearing his throat and raising his voice another octave, Yeshuah repeated his announcement. "My lord scribe, I bring you a message from Ezekiel the High Priest."

"Since when did I become 'my lord scribe,' and when did Ezekiel become High Priest?" Zadok asked.

"The council met last night and conferred the title upon him. In his acceptance of the office, he insisted to the council that you be made his official scribe. It is a great honor. The council continues to meet. He wishes to see you at once to confirm, in their presence, that you will accept."

Hearing this, Miryam bowed with an exaggerated flourish. "You must go and accept this great honor, my lord scribe. Please make sure you are back before sunset, my lord scribe, so you can finish thatching the roof, my lord scribe." She couldn't restrain herself and burst into a fit of laughter.

"Please inform Mar Ezekiel, *Hacohein Hagadol*, that I shall be along presently as soon as I can assure the wife of the lord scribe that the lord scribe's roof is not leaking. His official scribe wants to make sure that when his meeting with the High Priest is over, he will be returning to a dry house and a happy wife."

Miryam's laughter continued, but she was still able to invite Yeshuah into the house and out of the rain for some modest refreshment. "Zadok, you should have enough fronds to finish the job."

In the time it took Yeshuah to eat and drink, the rain stopped, and night was rapidly approaching. After finishing his meal, he came back outside and needled Zadok repeatedly about getting underway to Ezekiel's house.

Zadok took his time and did as well as a scribe could be expected to do finishing thatching the roof.

With the task finally complete, Zadok washed his hands and face with cold water from the basin next to the front door. He entered the house, changed into dry clothes, and collected his winter cloak. At last, he was ready to leave. He bade Miryam farewell, and she bowed again and laughed.

Yeshuah, eager to fulfill his mission, led the way.

Zadok walked about as fast as Yeshuah rode wobbling from side to side on the long-suffering ass. The journey took all of ten minutes.

As Zadok approached Ezekiel's house, he saw a crowd gathered around the entrance to the small front garden. "What's going on, Yeshuah? Is something wrong? Is Mar Ezekiel not well?"

"You are a worrier, my lord scribe. The community has joined the council to congratulate our new High Priest."

Yeshua dismounted and strode through the open gate with Zadok following.

More members of the community and several Judean priests were standing by the front door. They parted to allow Zadok and Yeshuah to pass.

Ezekiel, upon seeing Zadok, rose to greet him, a proud smile on his face. "Zadok, my scribe, my son! Thank you for coming so soon. I need you to get started."

"Get started doing what, Mar Ezekiel?" Zadok asked, taken aback by all the commotion.

Rushing forward, placing himself between Zadok and Ezekiel, Yeshuah announced, "You will address the *Cohein Hagadol* before the council with proper respect."

Zadok stared at the portly priest. "Yesterday, my mentor was Mar Ezekiel. Today he is the *Cohein Hagadol*. It will take a while for me to get used to the idea, Mar Yeshuah."

"May the *Cohein Hagadol* speak for himself?" Ezekiel asked, frowning at the fawning priest.

"Of course, my lord." Yeshuah replied as he backed away.

Ezekiel smiled at Zadok. "My boy, as you are surely aware, your discovery of the *Mishkan Scroll* in the storeroom has changed everything. It is truly the hand of the God of our ancestors reaching out to us, showing us the true path, we must follow. Last night, when I read the scroll to the council of priests, their response was immediate and emphatic."

Interrupting Ezekiel, a shouted chorus of *"amein v'amein,"* arose from the council members standing around them in the room.

Ezekiel nodded to the priests and continued, "The elders recognized that, like the Israelites in the Sinai, we too are in a wilderness, the wilderness of our exile. For the Israelites, their *mishkan* was a visible sign of the presence of the God who set them free from bondage. It gave them hope and shored up their faith. The council, therefore, has agreed that we must build our own *mishkan* in this wilderness of Bavel. We must do it now."

Again, an *"amein"* chorus punctuated Ezekiel's fervent speech.

Zadok was impressed when he saw all the council members nodding in agreement. He thought, it was rare they agreed on anything. They appeared to be truly united in Ezekiel's mission.

Ezekiel pushed on, "The Council elected me *Cohein Hagadol, High Priest,* because it was necessary to have a unified leadership for this great task we have been called to perform. I cannot do this work without you at my side. Zadok, it is you who made it possible to maintain our scribal traditions. It is you who found the scroll. It is you I trust." He smiled again. "I need you as the official scribe of the *mishkan."*

Zadok lowered his head and spoke in a whisper. "What do I know about building a *mishkan?"*

Ezekiel lifted Zadok's chin so he could look into his eyes. He spoke to Zadok, but loud enough for all in the council to hear. "Ten years ago, the God of our ancestors sent me a young boy who rescued the sacred scrolls of our people. That young boy taught us to cherish the words of Moses. That same boy, now a man, found yet another sacred scroll that shows us the way to keep our nation together."

Zakok was embarrassed by this praise. It was God that chose him for this work.

Laying his hands on Zadok's shoulders, Ezekiel continued. "There will be so many tasks, records to keep, letters to write and copy. Zadok, you must accept this great honor. Our entire community needs your talent and skill to assure our survival. We know there will come a day when we shall return to Judah and Jerusalem. In the meanwhile, the *mishkan* will hold us together and keep us ready for our redemption. I need your help."

Zadok hesitated and then asked, "My lord High Priest, our community is practically starving. How can we pay for such a structure? The *Mishkan Scroll* describes the construction of the sanctuary in great detail. There are enormous quantities of gold and silver called for in the design. Where are we supposed to amass these materials? The Bavlim have already forbidden us the construction of our own Temple in exile. They have restricted the areas in which we might build our homes. What makes you think they will allow us to build this movable *mishkan?* Do you actually intend to move it from place to place in this country of exile?"

Ezekiel cast Zadok a broad smile. "Which question shall I answer first, Zadok? If the hearts of Israel are willing, just as described in the scroll, we shall have, like Moses, more materials than we can use."

Zadok remained doubtful.

Ezekiel continued, "You know as well as I do, that some of our fellow Judeans have, despite our low status, prospered in this exile. We shall insist that these fortunate ones actively participate in the building of the *mishkan*. We shall convince them that not to do so would be bad for their business. As for the likely response of the Bavlim, I have spoken with the *Pehcha*, the Governor of our district. He promised to take our request directly to the King. He even offered to transport the *mishkan* on his barges, for a fat fee of course." He smiled. "Did I mention that the *mishkan* will be floating on the rivers of Bavel? I am sure Moses, in his own day, wished there were rivers in the desert."

In spite of all of his doubts, Zadok was beginning to see the need for the *mishkan* as a way to bring hope to his people. Looking at Ezekiel's determined expression, as he addressed the council, Zadok realized that his mentor was counting on his support. He turned and faced the council. "I am honored to accept your confidence in me and shall do whatever I can to make the vision of the God of Moses come true."

The members of the council rose and surrounded Zadok and Ezekiel with warm embraces and expressions of support for the *mishkan*.

And so it was, that Zadok, son of Achituv the Scribe, agreed to High Priest Ezekiel's urging and became the Chief Scribe of the Judeans in exile, and overseer of the work on the *mishkan*. Though he felt honored to be trusted with this sacred task, he knew there would be many obstacles that might frustrate God's will. He prayed he was up to the challenges ahead.

CHAPTER NINE

DATE: March 17, 2009
TIME: 3:30 P. M. Local Time
PLACE: Step Down Unit, Souraski Medical Center, Tel Aviv

Malik began to pace the hospital room again, thinking aloud. "The killers may indeed be Samaritans. They may even believe that they are doing this as part of some deal with Hamas. But I suspect there is another hand being played, by a yet unknown interested party. So far, that party has been content to watch, as official heat is applied to the *Shomronim.*"

"So, who is playing this hand?" Stone asked.

Malik helped himself to a bottle of water on the table. "I would put my money on the person or persons who are currently in possession of the scroll. And just so we are clear, I do not believe it to be the Samaritans. Nor is it Hamas. They would have exploited it by now. No, it must be someone who can actually read the scroll and decode it."

"Then we need to go back to the theft of the scroll itself." Lt. Colonel Lavi said. "At this point in our investigation, Gadi Sagal, an employee of the Hebrew Union College is the prime suspect. We need to start with him."

Rafi nodded his head in agreement. "Colonel Lavi, you and Sergeant Ramon get up to Jerusalem and see what is being done to locate Sagal and the scroll."

"Who died and left you in charge?" Keller asked.

"Actually the Defense Minister put me in charge. Would you like his mobile number to confirm my orders?"

Keller was dubious. "You have his cell phone number?"

"On speed dial, Sergeant Keller. We are a small country. We are like a big rambunctious family. The Minister has taken a personal interest in this matter. Actually, your Secretary of the Navy phoned your Secretary of Defense who in turn phoned our Minister of

Defense and asked what we were doing to protect American Naval personnel while on leave in Israel. We told him it was complicated. I was assigned to lead this band of warriors and 'uncomplicate' things. Your safety is now my responsibility."

Rafi pressed on, "Keller, you, Rabbi Stone, and Colonel Malik will work on decoding your copy of the Ezra text. Any results you achieve, you will share with me via text message. Here is my number. Put it into your phone, then destroy this card."

Keller reluctantly accepted the business card.

Rafi turned to Malik, "Colonel Malik, are you able to handle a couple of last-minute house guests? They will be safer in your home than in a hotel."

"It shall be my honor. My late wife, of blessed memory, always accused me of trying to turn our home into a *pensiyon*. That's like what you call a bed and breakfast in the States."

Rafi turned to Omar and said, "Omar, be so kind as to loan Sergeant Keller one of your Berettas. I will feel much better knowing that the United States Marines are providing security for our scholars."

Omar reached down to the ankle holster strapped to his right leg, drew the Beretta, and passed it, handle first, to Keller. "Be careful with her, Sergeant. She is a good friend."

Keller hefted the weapon and placed it in his pocket.

Rafi looked sternly at Keller. "Sergeant, in case anyone asks, you did not get the weapon from us. You found it in a dumpster in Jaffa. It is, as you Americans say, clean. It cannot be traced to anyone. Need I remind you that it is only for your defense and nothing else?"

Keller patted the weapon in his pocket and nodded.

Rafi turned next toward Lt. Stone. "Rabbi, as far as this hospital is concerned, you were never here. If for any reason you need the medical records of your stay, you will please contact Dr. Benyoshua directly."

"I understand," Stone said.

"Meanwhile, I would like to bring this group together again in twenty-four hours to see where we are in all of this. Let's meet at the Department Store at this time tomorrow. Agreed?"

"What's the Department Store?" Stone asked.

"I'll explain it to you later when we get settled at my home," Malik said.

Keller shot an annoyed glance at Stone. All this 'hush-hush' stuff was not getting him closer to his scroll. He was glad when the meeting finally broke up at 4:40 p.m. He still was not completely sold on Malik being trustworthy. He needed to learn more about this Colonel Malik, but how?

Malik's tan Opel was parked in the far corner of the parking lot restricted to emergency room patrons. The windshield was covered in notices that the space he had parked in was reserved. Malik tossed them into a nearby trashcan.

Keller walked around the car, his hand on the metal body.

"Is something wrong Sergeant?" Malik asked.

"Not really, unless you count tiny bomb fragments embedded in the hood and doors as 'wrong.' Your car was about as lucky as you were." He eyed Malik.

"Thank you for your concern. I would not have a car had I not parked it around the corner from the tea shop."

"How far is the nearest *Hamashbir?*" Stone asked.

Keller turned to Stone. "What is *Hamashbir?*"

Stone started to gather her belongings and put them in the plastic bag supplied by the hospital. "It's a department store. When Rafi mentioned something about a Department Store, I decided I would not spend another minute in these borrowed scrubs. You should consider a shopping trip of your own."

Malik replied, "There is a store less than five minutes from here and it's even on the way to my home."

Keller scowled at his soiled shirt. "Are they open? Do they have men's clothing?"

Malik smiled. "Was Ezra a scribe?"

The brief ride to the department store ended in success. Rabbi Stone emerged from the women's wear department dressing room sporting the Israeli version of the L.L. Bean look: dark khaki cargo pants, white cotton blouse, navy blue V-neck cotton sweater, Teva sandals. When she rode the escalator down to the main floor, she encountered Keller about to ride up.

Malik laughed at their startled expressions. Then Keller and Stone joined in.

Customers passing by the three laughing shoppers could not see what was so funny. A few shook their heads as if the three were lunatics.

Keller was astonished. They were both dressed in identical outfits, right down to the sandals. "You have great taste, Lieutenant," he said, a broad smile on his handsome face.

"So, do you," Stone replied, admiring Keller's taut physique.

Malik smiled. "I would say that it looks like the two of you were meant for each other," he said.

Stone raised her shopping bag as if she was about to clock him with it but was smiling.

Malik's home on Jabotinsky Street, was the left side of a Bau Haus style duplex, a couple of blocks from the beach, in Tel Aviv. After years of neglect, this section of the first modern Jewish city in Palestine was receiving a makeover by Israeli yuppies who discovered that these old buildings with curved shapes and smooth lines were historically and practically very valuable.

As they mounted the front steps, Keller could see into the window of a turret-shaped front room.

Malik unlocked the front door and let them in.

The soft glow of a pair of lamps revealed a colorful rug in an abstract pattern centered on a cream-colored terrazzo floor. The rug might have been mistaken as the aftermath of a Picasso and Chagall paint fight. A flat, highly polished wood desk stood against the front window looking out on the street.

Malik said proudly, "Welcome to *beit* Malik! Let me show you around and get you settled, then we can have a bite to eat. You must be starving. I am not the cook my Aviva was. May her memory be for a blessing. But I can prepare frozen soup with the best of them."

"Thank you, but I'm not hungry," Stone said.

"Perhaps later." Malik pointed out the location of the bathroom on the first floor and the guest room on the other side of the wall, also facing the street. "I'm sorry, but the only light in here is provided by the reading lamps attached to the bed. Rabbi, you should be comfortable here."

"Stop worrying. If I can make do with a rack on an aircraft carrier, I can survive a down comforter. I'll be fine," Stone said.

"Silly me, of course." Malik turned to Keller. "Sergeant, you will have to make do on the leather couch next door. I will bring you some sheets and towels. Feel free to draw the curtains. We don't want our neighbors getting too excited. I will have some soup going in a moment."

Malik left to get their meal underway.

Stone and Keller dropped their backpacks in their assigned rooms and joined the professor in his kitchen.

Keller was surprised to see how modern the kitchen was. He shook his head. Everything was bright red: cabinets, refrigerator, and stove were all the color of a fire engine, he thought.

True to his word, Malik was dumping a couple of frozen soup blocks into a pan of boiling water. In a few moments, the soup's fragrance filled the kitchen, an aroma of beef and barley and assorted vegetables. From a bread drawer, Malik pulled out a loaf of hard crust rye. He cut the loaf into one-inch-thick slices and placed them in a white plastic breadbasket. Out of the refrigerator came a tub of unsalted butter and a jar of Israeli strawberry preserves.

Keller wondered if Abby was now as hungry as he felt.

Malik disappeared for a moment and then reappeared with two wine bottles in hand. "This is the finest vintage from the Golan. Are you permitted to drink from the produce of the occupied territories?" He chuckled. "I am joking, of course."

Keller examined the label. "I could go for some Tennessee sour mash right now, but since that does not appear to be an option, this wine will more than compensate. I won't tell the State Department if you won't."

Malik turned to Abby. "And you, Rabbi Stone, may I pour you a glass?"

"By all means, Professor. It is exactly what I need on top of the painkillers from the hospital. I should be able to sleep like a baby."

As they ate, Keller wanted to learn more about what Stone, and he could expect. He sipped at his wine and asked, "Professor, what is the deal with this so-called 'department store?' Rafi said we are supposed to meet up there?"

Malik lowered the glass from his lips. "You must both be exhausted. I'll explain in the morning. Meanwhile, we could all use a good night's sleep." He rose from his chair. " *Lailah tov, my friends,*" he said.

Keller wondered why Malik ended the conversation so abruptly. He saw Abby could barely stay awake. "Malik is right. You need a good night's rest."

Abby yawned. "At least, we are safe here," she said and let Keller guide her to the guest room. "With my American Marine on the couch, I shall sleep very well. Lailah tov."

Keller thought of giving her a quick goodnight kiss, but this was not the right time or place. He heard Abby's door click shut and reluctantly let his body drop onto the couch. He fell asleep immediately.

Keller did not know what time it was when he became aware of someone standing over him. Very slowly, his right hand reached for the 9 mm. Beretta he had placed under the sheets at his side.

"You won't need the gun, Sergeant." Stone's voice was soft.

Keller sat up. "Are you OK? What's wrong?"

"I---I need a friend. Come with me." Stone extended her hand.

Keller stood up and took her hand in his. Suddenly, he became aware that he was only in his undershorts. He quickly withdrew his hand and grabbed the sheets for some cover.

"That is so cute," Stone said. "I would very much appreciate it if you would join me in the guestroom. I don't want to sleep alone."

"Is that an order, ma'am?"

"Would it help if it was?"

"It wouldn't hurt."

"I don't want you to do anything you are not comfortable with."

"Truthfully, I've been imagining a moment like this since we met on the Roosevelt."

"Imagining or fantasizing?"

"Works for me either way. I just want to make sure that I'm not going to be drummed out of the Corps for conduct unbecoming."

"Let me put it this way, I need you at my side because I am having vivid flashbacks of the explosion. I can't get myself to close my eyes, but I desperately want to sleep." Abby smiled sadly. "There is no guarantee that you sharing my bed, will lead to conduct unbecoming."

Keller looked disappointed.

Abby smiled. "Look, I'm not saying it couldn't happen, but I'm not promising either. Besides, I am the one who can be brought up on charges of sexual harassment, not you. You are at my mercy, so to speak."

"I'm beginning to see the possibilities here."

"I thought you would."

"Is there any chance I could address you as Abby and you call me Ron? Sergeant, Rabbi, and Lieutenant kinda inhibit the likelihood of there being conduct unbecoming."

"You, smooth talker, Ron. I'm tired. Come to bed."

"Aye, Aye, Abby."

Malik sat at the top of the stairs a huge smile creased his weathered face. *That went well,* he thought to himself. Whatever happens next, that went well.

CHAPTER TEN

DATE: Second Day of the First Month, In the Thirteenth Year Since The Destruction of Jerusalem
TIME: First Hour of the Third Watch
PLACE: Beside the River Frat, Site of the *Mishkan* Project

Nearly three years had passed since Zadok was named Chief Scribe and accepted Ezekiel's appointment to lead the *mishkan* project. Zadok took to his task like a general preparing for battle. Victory would be in the details. Pulling together the materials and overseeing the elements of its design were not difficult. His greatest challenge was moving the sanctuary from place to place. Ezekiel envisioned the *mishkan* floating on the water in a barge. But where was it supposed to land? Today, Zadok set out to find Ezekiel and push for answers. He did not have to look very hard.

Ezekiel was already on his way to meet with Zadok and learn how the project was going. Zadok welcomed the High Priest into his work tent. "My lord High Priest, I have an idea you need to consider."

Ezekiel surveyed the tables and piles of papers lying about. "Speak, Zadok. That's why I came, to see how things are progressing."

Zadok rummaged through a pile of papers. Frustrated, he could not locate the map he wanted, he threw the documents into the air.

Ezekiel placed his hand on Zadok's arm. "Zadok, calm yourself. Tell me what the problem is, and we'll figure it out."

Zadok stared at his mentor. "I am worried. I do not know where we will erect the *mishkan* when it stops on its journey? The transport barge must be large. Will we be able to get it close enough to the shore to safely unload the Sacred structure?" He shook his head. "It would be a disaster if, after all our hard work, we could not unload the house of God safely. Imagine if it landed in pieces in the river?"

Ezekiel frowned. "You are right as always. What do you suggest? Knowing you, as I do, I am certain you have given these problems a great deal of thought."

Zadok finally located the map he was searching for and spread it on the table. He traced his finger along the path of a wide river. "I will need to travel the river *Frat* to scout out acceptable landing points."

Ezekiel shook his head. "You are too valuable here. Someone else should be sent."

Zadok turned toward his mentor. "I am afraid I am the only one I would trust with this mission. I alone know our precise requirements."

Ezekiel smiled sadly. "If this is how you feel, then go ahead and do it. You are in charge. I have faith in you."

"I too wish there were another way," Zadok said.

Ezekiel nodded. "Get the Bavlim to help you. It is important that we do this in the right way. The Bavlim do not like surprises."

The journey on the river *Frat* took Zadok three weeks. The landing sites he chose were positioned on level patches of ground just above the water's edge, at the spring flood high watermark. The sites were large enough to accommodate the *mishkan* and those who would gather to it. Zadok recruited local Judean exiles to properly prepare the sites.

When Zadok returned to Pumbedita, he reported to Ezekiel, showing him on a map of the river, the landing locations he had chosen. Ezekiel then met with the *Pecha*, the local Bavli governor. After answering many pointed questions and a great deal of discussion, he received imperial permission to erect the *mishkan* at the designated sites.

Zadok had learned a great deal about the river and landing sites. Now back home, he realized the landing closest to Pumbedita required more work than all the rest. He had Judean workers gather at all hours of the day, between dawn and dusk, to clear away the dense reeds and canes that grew along the river. At times, it felt as if every Judean exile in Pumbedita was engaged in the task. He wondered if it would ever be completed.

Each day, Zadok surveyed the site, as reeds and grass fell where they were cut by the teams of workers. He ordered heavy ox carts and wagons to roll back and forth to flatten the ground and help dry it out. Finally, after a month of back-breaking work, a square flat area broad enough for a grand palace greeted his eyes.

A week later, the Pumbedita landing site was ready. With a large smile on his face, Zadok faced the workers. "My brothers and sisters, it is time. Go back to your workshops and homes and gather the components. Thanks to your skill and labor, we will begin to raise up our dwelling for the God of Judah and Israel, today, here."

As the first vertical wooden posts were set in place and tied to horizontal members, the men lashed gold fittings upon them. These gold pieces sparkled in the strong light before sunset, shooting off brilliant rays in all directions. Zadok was now ready to present the *mishkan* to the council. The council was scheduled to meet in Pumbedita in two days.

It was a mild spring day, clear and warm, but Zadok was perspiring as if it was the middle of summer. He shuffled the sheets of papyrus into alignment and were all beneath the shade of a large goat's hair canopy that normally served as Zadok's workspace. Zadok looked out at the twenty-four members of the council seated before him. Ezekiel sat centered in the front row. The members were able to look past Zadok and see for themselves the *mishkan* being assembled before them.

Zadok straightened himself and cleared his throat. "My lord, *Cohein Hagadol*, members of the Council of Judah in Exile, as you have requested, here is my comprehensive report on the *mishkan* project."

A voice from the council called out. "Zadok, is this report going to be longer than the *Mishkan Scroll* itself?"

The Council members responded with laughter. A few shushed the disrupters.

Zadok waited for silence. Then he cleared his throat. "From the moment you authorized the building of the *Mishkan*, nearly three years ago, the response of our community to the call for skilled craftsmen and laborers was amazing. As you are well aware, the *Mishkan Scroll* fanned the fading embers of our tribe-in-exile, into a blaze of national pride. With each passing day, we were able to add names to the rolls of Judean artisans accepted for work on the Sacred sanctuary." He looked up from his notes and added, "It may interest you to know that some of those artisans were old enough to have been employed in the Sacred House in Jerusalem. They came to us with elaborate examples of their workmanship. The pieces they offered were truly beautiful."

Ezekiel beamed up at his Chief Scribe.

Zadok continued, "As directed by the Council and the High Priest, my assistants and I have kept close accounts of the materials donated and employed throughout."

A council member in the front row stood and addressed Zadok. "Is it true that your wife is one of your scribal assistants?"

"Yes, it is true." Zadok was proud of Miryam's skill and devotion to their task.

"Is that wise? Who takes care of your children?"

Zadok did not anticipate this kind of question. "Miryam, my wife is a very skilled scribe. When I am not available to provide answers to questions on the meaning of specific instructions from the *Mishkan Scroll,* Miryam is more than able to do so. My sons assist their mother in the little tasks that can be done by children. They are not neglected."

The man was still standing, so Zadok began to shuffle his notes, trying to conceive an answer that would satisfy the council member.

"Dear Husband, perhaps I may be able to assure the council member of my worthiness to work on the project." Miryam continued to speak as she walked briskly from the rear corner of the tent to stand next to Zadok.

Zadok's face reddened and he became flustered. "Miryam, have you been here the whole time?"

Ignoring Zadok, Miryam looked at the questioner directly. "I have been overseeing the weavings for the *Mishkan.* This work took place in individual homes. Most of the weavers were women. When a section was completed, it was brought before the priests for their approval and then to me. I made a small mark in ink on one corner of each item to assure, that no one attempted to receive payment for the same cloth twice. Once recorded and marked, the cloth was returned to the weaver for storage. As you can now see, all the pieces are being brought together for assembly."

Zadok smiled. "So, my wife's work has been important to our success."

The man, still looking doubtful sat down.

Zadok nodded to Miryam and continued, "It is exciting that metal objects have been fabricated in villages throughout Bavel. As these were completed, they were presented to the priests and my scribes to be recorded."

Ezekiel stood. "Tell the council, my son, how the *Mishkan Scroll* guides our work."

Zadok reached inside his tunic and withdrew a scroll.

There was a gasp from the council. One council member rose and shouted, "Is that how you treat a sacred scroll? Why is it not secured under guard?

Several members of the group murmured their agreement.

Zadok shook his head. "My lord council members, the *Mishkan Scroll* is not an object of worship. It is the constant guide for our work. We need to be able to always refer to the text. It answers questions and provides information to help us make our decisions." He looked kindly at the concerned faces. "Every time I open this scroll, it becomes more precious to me. I ask myself which of our sacred ancestors held this scroll in his hands? How did they feel when writing down the words of Moses?"

Many members of the Council nodded their heads to show agreement.

Half an hour later, Zadok felt he answered most of their questions. When would it be enough?

Ezekiel rose and turned to the council. "Thank you all for coming. That is all the talk for today. Perhaps now you would like to see the *Mishkan* up close."

Zadok sensed the excitement as Ezekiel adjourned the meeting.

Zadok felt exhausted as the council members took their leave. He knew the High Priest was pleased with his report but worried the others might not be totally convinced. And then, what was Miryam thinking, interrupting his report? It was now time for him to focus on the details of the consecration of the *Mishkan.* Judah in Exile was about to be united by a movable sanctuary on the banks of the waters of Bavel. Despite the clear guidance of the *Mishkan Scroll* and the hearty endorsement of Ezekiel and the council, Zadok still had his doubts. Was this truly what God wanted? How would he know? What if something went wrong?

CHAPTER ELEVEN

DATE: March 18, 2009
TIME: 10:30 A.M. Local Time
PLACE: Babylonian Jewry Heritage Center #83 Mordecai Ben Porat Avenue
Or-Yehudah

Gunnery Sergeant Aaron Keller was quite pleased with his performance on the bed of battle, entangled in combat with Lieutenant J.G. Abby Stone. There were a series of skirmishes, each ending in exhaustion and brief periods of sleep before the battle was joined once again. In Marine combat training, repetition is a key aspect of Corps doctrine. If you performed an action enough times in training without the stress of actual combat, your body would perform properly under the worst of battlefield conditions. *Got to love that Corps doctrine*, Keller thought.

Although he had no trouble wrapping his arms around Abby's beautiful body (who knew she was so well put together under all that camouflaging clothing?) Keller could not wrap his arms around the fact that he just had rough and tumble, sweaty sex with his rabbi. He may have joked about his religious beliefs with friends and family, but being in bed, naked, with Abby's head against his chest, put him in a questioning theological mood. *Is it a sin to fuck your rabbi? Is it a greater sin if you really, really, enjoyed it? What does it mean if you get another hard-on while having these spiritual thoughts?*

Abby was not actually sleeping in Aaron's arms. She was, as Fagin put it in the musical, *OLIVER*, "reviewing the situation." Unlike Aaron, her first thought was directed toward how good she felt, emotionally. Physically, she was still feeling the after-effects of the bomb blast. What Aaron might have interpreted as moans of pleasure and orgasm were in fact, cries of pain each time a blast-induced bruise was touched, or a sore muscle was stretched. She ached throughout her entire body.

Emotionally, Abby felt no guilt, no second thoughts about having great sex with a grunt Marine. There were times on board the Roosevelt when she believed she understood the celibacy of Roman Catholic nuns. It was, indeed, a choice. Shipboard romances are not confined to cruise ships. The sexually integrated Navy was a flotilla of casual sex. Dozens of officers including fighter jocks and wardroom adjutants found her very attractive. In ways subtle or crude, they let her know they would be honored to shtup her in a shaft alley or the anchor windless anytime she felt the urge. And she did have urges. She simply made a decision, that casual sex was not for her. Sex would be her decision on her terms with the man she chose. Keller was even Jewish. Her mother would be pleased. Her father would rather not know about any of this.

Aaron felt Abby stirring. "Did I hurt you last night?" He asked, eyes tender.

"No," she lied. "Thank you for your concern."

There was an awkward silence, broken when Aaron asked, "I'm curious. Why did you become a rabbi?"

"Why did you assume I was awake before?"

"Don't dodge the question."

Abby sighed. "I became a rabbi because I knew that it would shock the hell out of my parents."

"Really? That's it?"

"It's a long story. I'm not sure you want to hear all the gory details."

"Try me."

"OK, but remember, you asked for it. Becoming a rabbi was just something that felt right for me. I had no idea how my parents would react. The day my letter of acceptance arrived from the seminary my mother was polite but wary. My father was in a state of disbelief. I think the whole becoming-a-rabbi thing came as a complete and total surprise to him."

"You surprised me too," Aaron interjected.

Abby smiled. "I have that effect on soldiers. Anyway, once my parents started to look around, they saw the women rabbis of the Chicago area and realized that they were doing okay. Most had families. That was one of their concerns. Even some gay rabbis had families."

"Gay rabbis?"

"Shhh. Female rabbis were respected in their communities and made a decent living. My parents even said that it was possible I might find a nice Jewish husband—maybe a doctor or a lawyer."

"Does that mean that a Marine Gunnery Sergeant was not on their wish list?" Aaron gave his best impression of a pout. "We make wonderful husbands…lovers."

Abby laughed. "Don't flatter yourself."

Aaron let out an exaggerated sigh. "Once you learned they were okay with you being a rabbi, then what?"

"Once my parents accepted my career choice, I did not experience the joy I expected. I felt caged, boxed into a life of conventionality."

Aaron looked puzzled.

"I could not stand the idea of being perceived as a member of the establishment, even the Jewish establishment."

"You don't strike me as anything but 'establishment.'"

"I don't look it now, but I spent my high school years in a perpetual state of rebellion, against everything."

Aaron vigorously shook his head. "I can't be in bed with a rebel. I represent the U.S. of A."

"You have no idea. In Ann Arbor, I tried every destructive behavior short of dropping out or failing in class. Those two options would have gone completely against my grain." She lowered her voice. "I even liked Freshman English."

"No! So, rebel, I mean, Rabbi, what happened when the Chicago 'flower child' arrived at the seminary?"

"I managed to rebel in non-rabbi-like ways. I pursued archeology as a major. My parents got that message quickly: there would be no congregational life for their daughter. I was not going to conform to their model-rabbi scenario. I was not going to be a 'hatcher, match-er and dispatcher,' as the saying goes."

"I never heard of that."

"In other words, I was not going to just officiate from 'womb to tomb,' with weddings in between. I wanted something different."

"So, you chose archeology. Did your parents give up on you?"

"They tried very hard to convince me that it would be possible to serve a congregation from Rosh Hashana to Shavuot (roughly September to June), and then spend my summers on archeological digs in Israel with the money I earned."

"That makes sense. How did that work out?"

"I gave it my best shot. Their plan for me seemed reasonable. It could have worked. A major problem was finding a congregation that would buy into my preferred schedule. With every job interview, it became crystal clear to me that the rabbinic selection committees were very impressed with my ability, compassion, intelligence, and commitment."

"Did they have any problems with your ego?" Aaron asked.

"I'll pretend I didn't hear that remark," Abby said. "It was equally apparent that the congregations believed they could remake me into their image of a rabbi who stayed and worked in the congregation during the summer."

"What nerve! What did you do next?"

Abby sighed. "For the first time in my life, I gave up." Not hearing Keller make any remarks, she continued, "At the end of interview season, on a May Friday morning, the congregations were supposed to announce their choices. I walked into the Dean's office and declared that I was withdrawing my applications."

"Just like that? Did the Dean accept your decision?"

"Yes, but—"

"Yes, but what?"

"The Dean invited me for a cup of latte at the neighborhood Starbucks. That cup of coffee and Karla Schlesinger's gesture saved me—"

"Who's Karla Schlesinger?"

"She was the Dean."

"Women can become Deans in a rabbinical school?"

Abby glared at Aaron. "Sergeant Keller, you may have survived your tour in Fallujah, but you better get with the program, or you will not survive this day with me."

"Please proceed, Rabbi."

"I really did not know the Dean that well. Schlesinger was ten years older than me. She told me a little about herself, informing me that she was a reserve chaplain in the United States Navy. She explained that she chose the chaplaincy, as a way of buying time before she 'settled down.'"

"She sounds a lot like you."

"She was. She still is. Schlesinger thought the Navy would organize her life and make all her mundane daily decisions. She said it did all of that and more. Then she said what was most valuable to her was that the Navy taught her how to separate the trivial from the important. World peace, she said, was important. Getting the right car to drive, or a bigger house with larger payments was not."

"I can agree with that," Aaron said.

"As I said that latte conversation changed my life. Rabbi Schlesinger was a woman who exuded self-confidence. She was smart, strong, independent, and capable, all the things I wanted to be. She painted a realistic portrait of Navy life for a woman rabbi. The negatives did not scare me. It was the challenge I was searching for."

"And the rest is history," Aaron said.

A soft tapping on the bedroom door ended the dialogue. "Uh, would either of you kids like some breakfast? We can have coffee and Danish here, or we can go out for something more substantial," Malik said, doing his best to make the whole situation seem perfectly normal.

"Thanks, Professor," Aaron responded. "I think we better stay indoors. We wouldn't want to press our luck with Samaritan bombers. Give us a few moments."

Before Aaron was finished speaking, Abby grabbed the top sheet and wrapped it around herself, leaving Keller exposed and cold. She turned her back on him and started to dress in the corner by the chair that held her clothing.

Aaron saw his clothing was in a heap, two steps from the edge of the bed. He glanced at Abby. "You should use the head first. I can wait."

"Why thank you, Gunnery Sergeant Suh," Abby said in an exaggerated southern accent. "That's mighty Christian of you!"

"We have lots to do. Move yo' *tuches*." Aaron's Yiddish pronunciation was worse than Abby's southern belle impersonation.

Malik greeted them in the kitchen, holding up, for their inspection, some sort of plastic kitchen gadget. "I'm sorry, but living alone as I do, I do not own a proper coffee maker. We'll have to make do with these filter contraptions."

"Actually, Professor, I prefer them to the hazards of measuring out coffee." Abby began to pour boiling water into the cone-like device that stood atop her coffee mug. A pre-measured packet of coffee wrapped in its own filter was at the bottom of the cone. She then poured a cup for Aaron.

Aaron tasted the dark brew. "Hey, this is not bad. What is this called in Hebrew?"

"*Ca-fee fil-ter*," Malik said.

"It's tough to know when Hebrew is Hebrew and when Hebrew is Hinglish." Aaron moved to the kitchen table and sat down.

"You'll get the hang of it...in a few years." Malik grinned and then turned serious. "I thought of something last night, as I tried in vain to get some sleep. Before the bomb went off at the tea shop, I said the scroll probably contained a hidden message."

Aaron put down his cup.

Malik nodded. "We need to go to my office at the museum. I know it still might be dangerous, but there are resources and references there which may help us decipher the Ezra scroll. We can't waste any more time. There are others probably following the same trail and they have a better copy of the text." He glanced at Keller. "Take your coffee with you, Sergeant. I will try not to turn too sharply."

Malik was securing his front door. Keller and Stone were descending the steps to the sidewalk when the roar of a powerful motorcycle caught their attention.

Keller saw two helmets, like shiny black marbles, reflecting the morning sun.

The driver, clad all in black weaved the cycle back and forth down the street. The passenger, also in black, suddenly raised a machine pistol, and fired at the trio on the steps.

Stone and Malik dove for cover the moment they saw the pistol raised.

The gun had a noise suppressor, so when the rider cut loose, the rapid succession of shots made more noise at the point of impact than when fired.

Keller, Beretta in hand, cautiously raised his head. He heard the cycles roar away. "Abby, are you OK? Professor, are you hit? What the hell was that? Did you get a look at them?"

Stone rose slowly from the sidewalk. looking from side to side, grim defiance on her face. "I'm okay. But I've had enough of this!" She glanced at Keller and then Malik. "A lot of good that Beretta is against a machine pistol."

Malik was already in the middle of the street, on one knee. He rubbed his finger on the pavement. "Sergeant, did you get off a couple of shots at our attackers?"

Keller frowned. "Frankly, I was just shooting blindly, like in most combat in Fallujah. I could have shot an innocent bystander. Why do you ask?"

Malik raised his hand and pointed his index finger at Keller. "You hit one of them. This is blood."

The local police arrived on the scene in moments. Malik asked to speak with their commander. When he finished, he returned to Keller and Stone. "We can leave."

"How did you manage that?" Stone asked.

"I explained a little about our situation, and then gave him Rafi's number. The rest is history. We will be safer at my office than sitting here on the street. Let's go before something else happens."

At his museum office, Malik began rummaging around in his lower desk drawer. He produced three thick juice glasses and a bottle of Haig and Haig that looked very old. "I knew I had something for emergencies. I am not, as a matter of habit, a daytime drinker, but I believe that our close-call this morning calls for a toast to life, if you know what I mean."

Neither Stone nor Keller voiced any objection to the early morning Scotch. It did seem to help to settle their nerves, despite Abby's involuntary shakes that sent the scotch sloshing around in the glasses. As the warmth of the alcohol reached their cores, they stood in silence.

Malik broke the silence. "I am anxious to get back on the trail of the Ezra Scroll." He rubbed his hands together. "If we throw ourselves into our work, it will help us to fend off the terrors of this morning. Sergeant, hand me the copy of the text on my desk."

Keller fetched the copy, curious as to what Malik was upto.

Malik taped the copy of the text onto a wall-mounted whiteboard, and then stood back. He stared at it in silence for what seemed an eternity. He then turned around and opened his top desk drawer. He withdrew a rectangular magnifying glass with a black plastic handle. He moved the glass back and forth over the text slowly. "This is no good. I can't see enough detail. I'm not sure what I'm looking at. I don't know if they are smudges or intentional markings." He removed the text from the board and without warning, walked to the door.

"Where are you going, Professor?" Stone asked.

"I am going across the street, to the school. I need to borrow one of their science class microscopes. Meanwhile, as long as you are here, you should browse the exhibits in the museum. You will find them very relevant to our mission."

Before either Stone or Keller could reply to Malik's suggestion, Malik was out the front door.

"I don't like this," Keller grumbled.

Stone pulled Keller to the door of Malik's office. "You heard the man. Let's take a look. My reason for seeking Malik out in the first place was to learn more about Babylonian Jewry. Here's our chance."

Keller still wasn't sure, but went along without complaint. He soon found himself totally absorbed in the exhibits. "Abby, is it my imagination or am I seeing a younger version of the professor in some of these displays?"

Stone grinned. "Maybe it's because to American Jews, all Iraqi Jews look alike."

"I heard that racist remark," said Malik, catching up with them in the room dedicated to the story of Iraqi Jewry before the Second World War. Gripped tightly in his left hand was a heavy-looking microscope. With his right hand, Malik pointed to a photograph of a dark-skinned, scrawny, pre-teen. "They all look like me because they are me. Not many family albums in our community survived the war."

"You were a cute kid," Abby said.

Malik turned on his heels and started walking briskly down the corridor, to his office. Over his shoulder, he shouted back at them. "The museum tour is over. Come on, *yeladim*, remember, we are in a race with the murderous *mamzerim* who have the scroll. We have much work to do."

Keller glanced at Abby. She trusts him. Do I?

CHAPTER TWELVE

DATE: Eighteenth Day of the First Month, In the Thirteenth Year Since The Destruction of Jerusalem
TIME: Two Hours After Sunset
PLACE: Beside the River Frat, Site of the *Mishkan* Project

For Zadok and Eliezer, the expected observance of Passover was the excuse they relied upon to postpone the consecration of the *mishkan* until the twenty-first day of the First month. They wanted nothing to prevent the Judeans-in-exile from attending in large numbers. They need not have worried. Only a few of the exiles took the trouble to celebrate their freedom from Egypt. What was there to celebrate? The quality of existence under the Bavli was only a few small levels above slavery. A quiet, modest meal with family, featuring unleavened bread was about all they could manage.

In those last days before the consecration of the *mishkan*, Zadok found himself with time on his hands. He decided to walk to his work pavilion to study the *Mishkan Scroll* one more time. He needed to make sure he had not missed anything. With daylight gone, the ancient parchment of the *Mishkan Scroll* was so dark in color as to be nearly illegible. The light of the single oil lamp that hung over Zadok's worktable was almost useless. Nevertheless, he studied each letter, again. He noted every detail, every arch, and curve, long and short line. Even now, the scroll was still a mystery to him. *This scroll was not copied by a true scribe,* he thought, observing there was little uniformity in the letters and spacing. It appeared to have been done very quickly. He was able to make out places where a knife or sharp edge was used to scrape off a letter and replace it with a correction. Another curiosity was that each time, he dragged his finger along the edge of the scroll, it came away with a dark stain. Could he clean the scroll?

Zadok remembered his days as an apprentice scribe, watching with fascination as his teacher in the Sacred House demonstrated how to clean a parchment scroll.

"Bread, Zadok. Remember to use bread. You break it into a piece you can hold comfortably in your hand and then you start to rub the parchment, like this." To his amazement, the parchment was cleansed, but the letters were not damaged. The text stood out sharply against the cleaner background. He wondered why this simple process had not been done with this scroll when it was first written.

Zadok decided to test the cleaning process himself. He found a piece of bread, left behind by one of the scribes at a writing desk. He spread the scroll out on his table, then selected an edge of the scroll and gently rubbed the bread on the dark parchment. The material looked brighter. Hopeful, he selected a section of writing near the beginning of the scroll. Hesitating, fearful of damaging the sacred letters, he gently rubbed the bread on a few words. He leaned over and studied where he had applied the bread. The scroll looked new...too new. An ancient scroll would darken with age. Dirt could be removed, but the parchment would naturally darken. No amount of rubbing would restore it to its original color. This was strange.

Zadok tried the experiment again with the same unexpected result. "It is too clean," he muttered. He stood back, dismayed by his discovery. The *Mishkan Scroll* was nowhere near as old as the other sacred scrolls. How was this possible? What did this mean?

For the moment, the excitement of completing the work of the *Mishkan* overwhelmed any misgivings Zadok had about the age of the scroll. He could be mistaken. There really was no way to establish the age of any parchment scroll. He needed to believe that the *Mishkan Scroll* was God's word to the exiles. Doubt faded to the back of his mind.

The *mishkan* in Bavel took two years and three months to complete. Zadok gained new respect for the abilities of the Israelites in the time of Moses. Those former slaves had managed the building of a moveable sanctuary in far less time. Perhaps the difference was the direct involvement of God.

Zadok began on the New Moon, working night and day, to copy and send out official invitations to Judean leaders all over Bavel, so that they would be able to arrive in time for the consecration on the twenty-first of the month. This would mark the first time since the destruction of the Sacred House in Jerusalem, that a large number of Judean exiles would gather together in one place.

Ezekiel made sure to obtain the permission of the rulers of Bavel for the dedication. Of course, they would be seated in places of honor. They would be invited to observe the ceremony from a special viewing platform erected outside the sacred precinct, but high enough to look over the site. Building the platform cost a fortune in labor and materials, but the High Priest was taking no chances. The continuing support of the Bavlim was essential.

Zadok knew that Ezekiel was very skilled at creating dramatic and powerful symbolic moments. If the *mishkan* was to serve as a unifying symbol of Judean redemption, it was important that as many of the exiles as possible be present for the consecration.

Three weeks before the consecration, Ezekiel assembled former Sacred House musicians near the assembly site of the *mishkan*. Ezekiel's network of informants made him aware that the surviving members of the Levite Guild of Sacred House musicians intended to challenge his authority as well as the *mishkan* project itself. Thus, when he gathered them all together and requested new music for the ceremony, he already knew what their answer would be.

Korach son of Izhar, and a respected musician, spoke for his fellow Levites. "My lord, High Priest. You know as well as we do that so long as the Sacred House is in ruins and Israel is in exile, we are not allowed to play our instruments for the worship of the God of our ancestors. That was our firm resolve as we stood by the waters of Bavel. We took an oath and the exiles bore witness to that oath. We will not sing, we will not play, until we are restored. We are bound by our sacred vow. The Eternal has not ended our exile. You have gone too far without the hand of the God of Abraham to guide you."

Ezekiel answered in an unusually soft voice. "I am grateful for your reminder and respect your sacred vows of loyalty to the Eternal One. Nevertheless, I ask you to take a good look around you. What do you see? They are your people. See what they have accomplished in this wasteland. Those loyal to the Eternal God have received instruction from Him and built a sanctuary for Him to dwell among us in exile. Is not their very success in building a true sign that the Eternal is with them and favors this work?"

Korach spoke with a clenched jaw. "We are sentenced to exile in this unholy land precisely because of kings and priests who arrogantly assumed that they knew what was in the heart of God. Now, you and your fellow blasphemers follow their evil ways. My family and I will await the true redemption of the God of our ancestors. We will have no part in this."

Korach and six of his sons and nephews stormed away from the *mishkan*. Zadok started to go after them. Ezekiel grabbed his cloak and pulled him back.

"Zadok, I do not in any way agree with them, but this consecration cannot take place by force."

Ezekiel tilted his head toward the thirty or so Levites standing out of the sun beneath a goat hair canopy. "We will work with the musicians who have remained. They understand how important this is for all of us." The followers of Korach did not disrupt the consecration.

***

People by the hundreds, celebrated their leader's accomplishment. Ezekiel extolled the *mishkan* as the nation's means of atonement for sin and their redemption from exile. It would be a symbol of their future return to Judah. Twelve oxen had been sacrificed on an altar of rough-hewn stones, one for each tribe, including the ten vanished tribes of Israel. As he supervised the priests making the first offering, Ezekiel pronounced a prayer that captured the deep emotions of the day.

"Let this offering hasten the return of the entire house of Israel to its people and its land. May the One who placed us here in exile, redeem us in our own lifetime." He thanked the Bavli officials profusely for their gracious permission to build the sanctuary and pledged the loyalty of the Judeans to the king of Bavel.

Korach, who heard these words from a distance, spat on the ground in disgust. He and his sons turned away from the celebration and began their return journey to their home-in-exile, up the river *Frat*.

Under Zadok's watchful eye, on the twenty-first day of each month, the *Mishkan* was packed up on a flat bottom barge and moved along the rivers of Bavel. Zadok was heartened that Judean exiles gathered wherever it stopped and participated in its re-assembly. In most instances, the assembly would be finished in time to celebrate the New Moon. At each river landing, Zadok would administer to the exiles an oath to abandon idolatry and worship exclusively the God of Abraham, Jacob, and Moses. Cohanim, trained by Ezekiel, would carry out the animal sacrifices. Music and singing would accompany the sacrifices.

Zadok was pleased to observe that, over time, Judeans ceased their attendance at the temples of Marduk and Ishtar. They were building a life for themselves in Bavel. Vineyards were planted, crops were sown, and herds of sheep and goats were maintained. He witnessed the people praising Ezekiel ben Buzi, their high priest. Zadok saw great improvement in their daily lives and attributed it to the presence of the *mishkan*.

In the months that followed the consecration of the *mishkan*, Zadok's life as Chief Scribe to the High Priest was hectic and filled with nearly impossible demands. There were benefits as well. Zadok's home had been enlarged and finally made watertight. His two rays of sunshine were his boys, who served the scribal schoolmaster as apprentice scribes. They reminded him of his own apprentice days in the Sacred House with his beloved brother, Eli. Each day he offered prayers of well-being for Eli and his family in Samaria. He believed that Eli was doing the same for him in Bavel.

Each year, on the anniversary of the consecration of the *mishkan*, seventy exiled priests of Judea would gather in Pumbedita for six days. The purpose of those meetings was to hear reports on the operation of the *mishkan* and how it was being received by the Judean people. As was the case in previous years, Zadok was expected to attend the meetings held in the courtyard of Ezekiel's home. As he passed through the gate, Zadok placed his hand on the gatepost for blessing. He reflected on how far both he and Ezekiel had come from their early days of exile. The home of the Judean High Priest had been completed the previous spring. It was the largest of all exile dwellings. The courtyard was spacious, easily accommodating the large number of priests attending.

This day's session was particularly tedious and of little consequence, or so Zadok believed. As always, Zadok attempted to make a complete record of the proceedings for Ezekiel. Almost too late, he realized that he did not have enough papyrus to make it to the end of the current session. Ezekiel told the priests to take a few moments for food and refreshment and they would resume as soon as Zadok retrieved enough papyrus for the task. He turned to his scribe and said, "Zadok, I think there might be some papyrus in my old workroom cabinet. You will find it on the middle shelf."

"I will be right back. Save me some figs," Zadok replied as he left for the workroom.

As Zadok expected, there was no papyrus on the middle shelf or any other shelf in the cabinet. Ezekiel was notorious for misplacing anything of importance or useful in his own home. He was about to close the cabinet when he noticed a few sheets of parchment in the back of the cabinet. Parchment was expensive and normally Zadok would not waste it on such a meeting, but without other options determined it would have to do. He was surprised but pleased that the parchment sheet on top of the pile was already prepared for writing. That would save precious time. The meeting had gone on long enough.

As Zadok lifted the sheet and began to roll it into a scroll, he noticed the sheet beneath it had writing on it. He picked it up. There was something familiar about the writing. He brought the sheet closer to the light of an oil lamp and gasped. He looked again and closed his eyes. Although the text was Aramaic, he was certain the writing was identical to that of the *Mishkan Scroll*. But this was not a sacred scroll. The content of this parchment sheet was a letter to a Bavli official. It cannot be, he thought. It cannot be.

Zadok read the writing again. He did not care about the message. He focused on the closing statement:

"I, Ezekiel ben Buzi, now swear an oath before the God of my ancestors, that all I have written here is the truth."

Zadok's hands shook. He was not mistaken. He was now convinced his first impression was correct. The letters of the words on this letter, preceding the signature, were identical to those in the *Mishkan Scroll*. The significance of his discovery was inescapable. His earlier suspicions began to make sense. Ezekiel, at the very least, was the copyist of the *Mishkan Scroll*. If that were the extent of his mentor's involvement, Ezekiel could have explained away the 'accidental' discovery of an 'original' scroll. But the high priest had gone to a great deal of trouble to make the scroll appear as an ancient document. In that instant, Zadok finally accepted in his bones that Ezekiel was the scroll's author as well. It had all been a fabrication by the priest. It was all a lie. That realization caused Zadok to immediately become violently ill. His stomach churned. His legs turned to liquid, and he collapsed in a heap on the floor.

CHAPTER THIRTEEN

DATE: March 18, 2009
TIME: 10:30 A.M. Local Time
PLACE: Babylonian Jewry Heritage Center #83 Mordecai Ben Porat Avenue Or-Yehudah

Stone, Keller, and Malik returned to the professor's office and Malik set the borrowed school microscope on his desk to examine the copy of Keller's mysterious document. The text was placed with great care on the stage below the microscope lens.

Malik bit his lip. "Sergeant, bring the desk lamp closer. I need more light. Aim it so the light shines from below."

Keller slid the brass, goose-necked lamp closer and positioned it as Malik requested.

"That helps. Thank you." Malik bent down over the scope.

"Well? What do you see?" Stone asked.

"Take a look," Malik said after several minutes of peering through the lens.

Stone bent her head over the eyepiece. Her right hand was on the focus knob. "What letter is this? I can't tell because the magnification brings it too close."

"It is an *ayin*." Malik replied.

"These shadows aren't smudges. They're *taggim!*" Stone muttered.

"What's that?" Keller asked.

"In the Jewish scribal tradition, they are called crowns," Malik said. "They are delicate, artistic, ornamentation, placed on the tops of letters. They only appear above certain letters. But this is all wrong."

Stone straightened up. "What is all wrong?"

Malik turned around to the whiteboard and picked up a blue dry-erase pen. He drew a line from one end of the board to the other, about two meters in length. "This horizontal line represents time. Since we are having this conversation in English, let us say that time begins here on the left edge." He drew a vertical line at the left edge of the board that extended about six centimeters above and below the horizontal line.

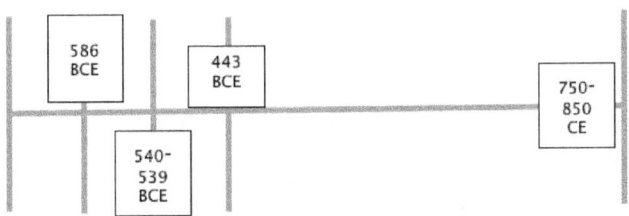

Keller followed Malik's every move. "Is that the Big Bang?" He asked, pointing to the first line.

"Bang, shmang. It is irrelevant. What matters are these vertical lines."

About half a meter from the left edge, Malik drew three vertical lines, each about ten centimeters apart and almost identical in length to the Big Bang line.

"This one represents the year 586 Before the Common Era. Judeans were taken into captivity by the Babylonians." As Malik said this, he wrote '586 BCE' above the horizontal line, next to the vertical. Pointing to the next vertical he then wrote, '540-539 BCE' below the horizontal line.

"What happened in that period?" Keller asked.

Malik pointed with the blue marker, "This line represents the year when Cyrus the Great of Persia allowed the Judeans to return to Judah." On the third vertical line from the left edge, he wrote '443 BCE.'

Malik continued, "This line, 443 BCE, is the date some scholars, including myself, believe Ezra read to the people from the Torah for the first time."

Malik then walked to the far-right edge of the board and drew a line and wrote the date, '750-850 CE.'

Stone studied the timeline. "I think I understand," she muttered.

"I'm glad one of us does," Keller said.

Malik pointed to the vertical line. "I will explain in a moment. This date, some twelve hundred years later, represents the first known appearance of *taggim*, the 'crowns' in a Torah text."

"So?"

Stone punched Keller lightly on the shoulder. "If I understand this correctly, it may mean that the Ezra text could be a forgery. Is that right, Professor?"

Malik let out a deep sigh. "Everything about it is wrong. Most scholars believe that *taggim* were created by the *Masoraim*—Masoretes."

Keller interrupted. "The who?"

Stone replied, "*Masoraim*. The name means something equivalent to, 'The ones who follow tradition.' They were Babylonian Jewish scribes from the seventh or eighth century of the Common Era, not BCE."

Malik smiled. "You remember. Very good. The Masoraim dedicated their lives to copying the Hebrew Bible with great precision. The consensus among Biblical scholars is, that these *taggim*, decorations, were intended to serve as reminders of various popular interpretations of the text."

"I don't understand," Keller said.

Malik sought a way to explain this. "The *Masoraim* were reluctant to actually change the sacred contents of the text. So, they invented a way to call attention to certain words. These crowns were like signals to interpreters. It was as if they were saying: 'Consider this word carefully. It means more than you might think.' As far as we know, *taggim* were used only for Torah scrolls."

Keller's brow was furrowed. "I seem to be missing something," he muttered.

Stone pointed to the whiteboard markings at the right end. "The earliest Masoraim were Jews from the seventh century of the Common Era. Let's say here." She pointed to the line. "There is no evidence of *taggim* before the beginning of that era and certainly, not on documents written in Paleo-Hebrew." When she saw Keller still looked puzzled, she added, "The location of your scroll is right, but the timing is off... by almost twelve centuries."

"Because the crowns were not used at that time," Keller said. "I think I get it."

Malik massaged his chin. "Maybe we should not be so hasty in our conclusions."

"What do you mean?" Keller asked.

"Well, consider this for a moment. There are no existing Babylonian documents or actual Hebrew texts of the Bible before the so-called earliest of the Masoretic texts. We do have the Dead Sea Scrolls, but most scholars agree that they were Judean, not Babylonian in origin. In fact, the discovery of the Dead Sea Scrolls revealed a highly organized Jewish religious community, never-before encountered in Judea." He eyed Keller. "Just because we have no actual evidence that *taggim* existed before the seventh century does not mean that they could not have been in use at that time. It is not impossible. It is just not provable." He looked at the timeline as he spoke. "What if the *taggim* were a long-standing Babylonian tradition, far older than we ever imagined? If the parchment is genuine, and the ink is appropriate to the fifth or fourth century BCE, we may still have the real Ezra scroll."

"Except for the fact that we don't have the Ezra scroll," Keller said. "Someone else has my scroll."

Stone shook her head. "Professor, I'm familiar with the tradition of *taggim*, but I have never seen *taggim* with so many points."

"Points?" Keller asked.

"Did you ever go deer hunting, Sergeant?" Stone shot him a teasing look, as if she was testing his testosterone level.

Keller smiled broadly. "A Carolina boy what don't hunt is a Carolina girl."

"Be careful, my sexist friend," Stone warned and laughed.

Malik looked from one to the other. "What in the name of heaven are you two kids talking about?"

"Deer, antelope, what-have-you, have racks of antlers on their heads. At least the males do, anyway." Stone picked up the dry-erase marker and drew a crude deer head with antlers. Her illustration of an antler had six tips, which she circled with a marker.

"You're a better rabbi than an artist," Keller shot at her.

Stone frowned. "Mr. Art Critic, even though these *taggim* look more like pine needles than crowns or antlers, these tips are like the points on a deer. If you look closely at the *taggim*, they have 'points.' Lots of them."

Malik returned to the microscope. "Ahhh...yes, you are quite correct. These *taggim* are unlike any I have seen before. Too many points." He shook his head.

"How many are too many?" Keller asked.

"I've never seen more than six or seven in any *Sefer Torah*," Malik said.

Stone counted the points on several of the taggim. "This letter has thirteen. The next fourteen, fifteen, sixteen, seventeen!"

"Tell me, which letters on this text have the crowns," Malik said.

Abby was still checking. "It looks like the same ones found in Torah today. *Gimmel, Zayin, Tet, Nun, Ayin, Tsadi, Shin...*".

Keller stared at the whiteboard and the diagrams of letters with *taggim*. "I have a crazy idea. Try to find the rack or letter with the greatest number of points."

"Good idea," Malik said. "You do it, Rabbi. You have younger eyes than mine."

Stone slowly shifted the copy of the Ezra text across the viewing stage of the microscope while counting aloud. "Twenty...twenty-one...twenty-two. So far none have more than twenty-two points."

"Are there still twenty-two letters in the Hebrew alphabet?" Keller asked.

"We can begin your Hebrew lessons later," Stone said. Right now, we don't have time for games."

"Really? Try this on for size," Keller said. "What if the pine needles, *taggim,* represent the letters of the Hebrew alphabet?" He saw a look of surprise on Stone's face. "The number of points could indicate which letter it stands for. Do we know if the order of the letters of the alphabet was the same back then as it is now?"

Stone stepped back from the board and stared at the notes that filled the dry-erase board. After a few seconds, a big smile crossed her face. "I will never refer to a Marine with the prefix 'dumb' ever again." She wrapped her arms around Keller's neck and kissed him on his lips.

Keller was stunned.

Malik laughed. "Sergeant, you just gave us the key to decoding the text. You did it!"

Keller gripped Stone around her waist. "So, it is like a code. It should be easy to break."

Malik shook his head. "Without the original scroll, our key has only entered the lock. It cannot open the door."

"I'm lost again," Keller said, releasing Stone.

Malik explained, "This copy is digital. There may be a few letters where the *taggim* stand out, but most appear as smudges or shadows. I am not even sure that some of the points we are counting are points at all. They could just be pixels. We cannot read the message behind the text until we have the original. Without that, we can be sure of nothing."

"Now what?" Stone asked.

Keller smiled, "That's simple. We find who has the scroll and steal it back."

Malik sighed. "Oy. If only it was that simple."

"It's time we arranged to meet our dear friends in the *Shin Bet*. I will make the call." Malik left his office and walked down the hall, opening his cell phone as he went.

Keller's gaze followed Malik. "Do you think he has the Shin Bet on speed-dial?"

Stone nodded. "They probably have him on their own speed dial list. Malik is quite a character for an old guy. We need to keep ourselves alert and ready for anything. Let's look at the text under the scope one more time."

Keller and Stone re-checked each letter that had the *taggim* embellishment, to make sure their initial impression was correct, that it conformed to the tradition of only certain letters carrying the crowns. By the time they had confirmed their thesis, Malik had returned.

Malik smiled and rubbed his hands together in anticipation. "The boys would like us to come to their office as soon as possible."

"Do we have to go?" Keller asked.

"Sergeant Keller, when the *Shin Bet* requests a meeting, it is best to comply," Malik said.

Keller sighed. "So, Colonel Malik of the MOSSAD, where is their office, exactly?"

"Women's Wear. Plus Sizes."

"I beg your pardon."

Malik grinned. "The top floor of *HAMASHBIR*, behind the dressing room for clothing designed for big women."

"You were in one," Stone said. "Remember where we got our current wardrobe? The department store. Still, it must look strange to other customers for all those toughs going into the dressing room to access the office."

"Some of our agents are women, you know. This is no time to be a sexist, Rabbi." Malik laughed. "For reasons that have as much to do with Jewish traditions of modesty as it does with ordinary self-consciousness, that part of the store is almost always deserted. When you look at fashion posters in this store, not one of them shows any image other than perfectly proportioned women. No one in this country wants to have themselves labeled as needing to wear plus sizes?"

Stone smirked. "Now who is being sexist?

Keller was skeptical. "How do you know all of this, Colonel?"

"When I was a much younger man, I was the one who came up with the idea of de-centralizing and locating our offices in ordinary places. *HAMASHBIR* was the first location of mine they accepted."

Stone shook her head. "Professor, you are a very strange man, indeed. Are you hiding any more secrets behind the old man disguise?"

"Rabbi, if I tell you..."

"I know---you will have to kill me. Ha, Ha."

After a ten-minute drive in Tel Aviv traffic, they parked across the street from their destination. This particular HAMASHBIR was easy to spot. The four-story cube stood out from its neighbors in the Tel Aviv shopping district. Malik, Keller, and Stone rode the central escalator to the fourth floor. As Malik had predicted, the floor was deserted. Each of them walked through the archway leading to the dressing rooms after making sure they were not being followed. Heavy green curtains covered a doorway at the rear of the dressing room area. Malik tapped twice on a steel door behind the curtains.

"Is that the Shin Bet secret knock?" Keller asked.

"We do not have a secret knock. If you were not supposed to be here, you would have been immobilized immediately upon stepping off the escalator. The whole store is wired for video. We have been monitored since we came through the front door." Just as Malik finished his description of security in the store, a loud metallic click sounded, and the metal door popped open.

Behind the door was a space so long that it ran along the entire side of the four-story cube. Omar, the Druse expert on the Samaritans, extended his hand in greeting. "Welcome to Plus Sizes! Follow me, and do not touch anything."

Keller saw that along the inside wall was a counter nearly thirty meters in length. Mounted on the wall above the counter were more than a dozen video monitors. Two young women were viewing the screens and manipulating control sticks. They carried on a conversation in low tones.

Stone could not make out all of what they were saying, but what she did catch did not sound like professionals screening for security threats.

Walking halfway down the length of the long main corridor, Omar opened a door and stood aside, ushering them into a small square room. A single, harsh fluorescent fixture lit up the area. A round wooden table, two meters across, was below the light. Five plastic stack chairs were arranged around the table. A disposable aluminum ashtray with three cigarette butts was the only 'decoration' on the tabletop.

Rafi appeared suddenly through a hidden door. "Have a seat." He joined them at the table.

When the group was settled, Rafi began, "I commend you on your discovery of a code in the Ezra scroll. Good work. However, it also means that the thieves are ahead of us because they have the original." He leaned slightly forward. "Let me be clear. I am not so sure the *Shin Bet* should even be a part of this adventure. Right now, it is merely a police matter. Attempted murder, and theft, are the only charges we could present at this time. Assuming we catch the bastards."

"Then why are we here?" Keller asked

Omar shuffled some papers in front of him. "It is the Samaritan angle that has us concerned. The bomb was so out of character for them. We are still trying to figure out if they are at the center of all this or bit players in someone else's drama. Until we get all these issues sorted out, we are going to partner with you to get the scroll back."

Rafi stood up and pointed a remote-control stick at a projector mounted to the ceiling. "For now, we need for you to take a look at something."

A screen dropped down from the ceiling in the front of the room. The screen was instantly filled with images of Tel Aviv street life.

Malik exclaimed, "That is the street outside the teashop. Based on the time stamp, this video was made just before the bomb blast. Yes?"

Rafi raised his hand. "Be patient, Professor. *Savlanut! Savlanut!*"

As if on cue, a motorcycle appeared on the left side of the screen and moved slowly down the street. The cyclist reached into a saddlebag on his right side and removed a parcel wrapped in black plastic and secured with silver duct tape. He placed it at the base of a concrete lamp pole and sped away.

Keller touched Abby's arm.

A brilliant flash of light obliterated the images on the street.

Keller felt Abby jump and saw her eyes close. He rubbed her arm gently.

After the violent explosion the video shakily revealed scenes of devastation and panic recorded by street cameras. There was an apparent editing cut in the video because the next image appeared to have been shot from a different angle, its focus on the end of a row of small stores. Amid the chaos on the street, Keller spotted a tall man standing partially hidden in a shop doorway. He was talking on a cell phone.

Rafi used the remote to freeze the image. "Do you recognize the man in the doorway?"

"I can't make out his...Oh – my– God! It's your archeology professor, Carlson," Keller said.

Abby sagged in her seat.

CHAPTER FOURTEEN

DATE: Twenty-Fourth Day of the First Month, In the Sixteenth Year Since The Destruction of Jerusalem
TIME:Two Hours After Sunset
PLACE:Beside the River Frat, Site of the *Mishkan* Project

A shadow hand placed a cold compress on Zadok's forehead. "Oh, Zadok, we were all so worried about you. You collapsed in the middle of Mar Ezekiel's writing room, after emptying your stomach all over his supply of parchment. You had such a high fever. It broke only last night. You have been sleeping continuously for two whole days."

Despite the haze in his mind, Zadok knew that the voice was that of his wife, Miryam. He recognized her gentle touch as well. Questions, so many questions swirled in his mind, like a whirlpool in the river. Was he overwhelmed by a bad dream, a nightmare that gave life to his doubts? Had he seen the letter written by Ezekiel's hand or was that part of the nightmare? Was the letter indeed written by the same hand as the *Mishkan Scroll?* He groaned as the full impact flooded his thoughts again. Was the entire *mishkan* project a huge lie, a fraud, put over on the exiles of Judah, playing on their desperate need for hope? The final thought shook him awake. Did Ezekiel realize that Zadok suspected the *Mishkan Scroll* was a forgery? "Has Mar Ezekiel been here?" he asked, trying to hide the alarm in his voice.

Miryam smiled. "Zadok, your friend has never left your side, except early this morning. There has been a tragedy. Well, perhaps not a tragedy, but the news is bad, nonetheless. Ezekiel was called away because his house caught on fire."

"Ezekiel's house?"

"It consumed everything he possessed."

"The sacred scrolls. What happened to them? Are they safe?" Zadok's mind was racing.

"Zadok, you are still delirious. You know very well that the sacred scrolls are kept at the school for scribes. They are safe."

"I need to see Mar Ezekiel at once! Get me some fresh clothing. Hurry!"

"Zadok, you are not strong enough to leave the bed."

"Just get me my clothes, please, Miryam. I must get to Mar Ezekiel's house now!"

By the time Zadok arrived at what had once been the entrance gate to the High Priest's Garden he was sweating and gasping from his exertion.

The stench of fire clogged the air surrounding the skeleton of the house. The work of the fire was complete. It was obvious that nothing of value remained. Nothing. Suddenly, he sensed someone behind him.

"Zadok, what are you doing here? Go back to bed and preserve your strength," Ezekiel said, his eyes on the charred ruins.

"Mar Ezekiel, is it...gone?"

"Look around you, Zadok. Everything is gone. Yes, even the *Mishkan Scroll*."

Zadok stared into Ezekiel's eyes, searching for any indication of animosity or loss of trust. Did the High Priest realize what Zadok had come to suspect? His patron's eyes revealed no emotion. His voice was soft and steady, as usual. It was impossible for Zadok to detect any change in Ezekiel's demeanor toward him.

"It is fortunate that you and your students were able to make copies of the *Mishkan Scroll*. We still have the text as a precious possession for our people." Ezekiel smiled at Zadok. "The original was consumed in the fire, but the *Mishkan* story still lives because of you. My possessions are gone, but no lives were lost. For that miracle, we should give thanks. Yes? Indeed, we should."

Zadok wanted to question Ezekiel about what he suspected. His courage failed him. He could not bring himself to confront Ezekiel with his suspicions, afraid of what the high priest might do to his family. What was Ezekiel capable of? The fire, he reasoned, was too coincidental. Was it an accident? Ezekiel might have guessed what Zadok had found that caused him to faint. He thought back to that terrible moment. *The letter...the letter with Ezekiel's signature...I left it lying on the writing table.* The fire conveniently erased any possibility that he could publicly accuse the High Priest of forging the Mishkan scroll. The proof that Ezekiel forged the text commanding the building of the Mishkan, proof that God did not order them to build this sacred house, was reduced to ashes strewn by the wind.

The impact of how far Ezekiel might go to protect his secret made Zadok dizzy. He grasped his walking staff for support. The entire *mishkan* project was a clever invention, a lie of enormous proportions. Ezekiel had used his imagination to create a myth about God wanting a moveable sanctuary in the wilderness. His motives may have been honorable, but his fraud, if discovered, amounted to blasphemy. Zadok stared at the remains of his mentor's home. He knew the truth would destroy all that he accomplished. But it was fraud. Sin. The flames on the altar of the *mishkan* consuming sacrifices meant to atone for the sins of the exiles were meaningless if God had not asked for them. Zadok shivered. What could possibly atone for his role in helping the blasphemous Ezekiel support the building of the *mishkan* in Bavel? He stared at Ezekiel and knew that only revealing the truth would cleanse his hands of the guilt he felt supporting the lie.

***

In the two weeks that followed the fire, Zadok watched Ezekiel closely. He sought to detect any lack of trust or hostility toward him. There was still no change in the High Priest's behavior that he could detect. It did not take long before Zadok concluded that the lack of change in their relationship might itself be an ominous sign. If Ezekiel was capable of burning down his home, he could easily conceal his doubts about Zakok. Why had he never questioned Zadok about the parchment letter on the table? *He must have seen it after I left it there when I fainted.* There were no questions asked and there no explanations offered. For Zadok, the uncertainty was physically debilitating and spiritually draining. He could not go on like this. He decided he would confront Ezekiel as soon as possible and ask him outright if he was the author of the Mishkan Scroll? He understood the risks but could not assuage his conscience and anger at being tricked into supporting the high priest's fraud. He viewed it now as an ambitious ploy to seize power in the name of God. How could he be silent with what he knew?

A few days later, in Zadok's work tent, an opportunity to be alone with Ezekiel presented itself. The other scribes left to prepare for the Sabbath. Zadok was clearing away his work when he saw Ezekiel enter.

Ezekiel gave Zadok his usual smile but was silent.

Zadok felt as if the priest was waiting for him to say something. He knew this was the moment. Afraid of the consequences, he cleared his throat and said, "My lord, High

Priest, I must ask you a question. It is a painful one for me. I have had many sleepless nights because of it."

Ezekiel looked Zadok over carefully and focused on his eyes. "Zadok, what is bothering you? Just ask me. Whatever it is we can work it out."

Zadok rushed it out. "Did you write the *Mishkan Scroll*?"

"Of course, I did!"

Zadok was stunned that Ezekiel admitted it so readily. "Then you do not deny it?"

Ezekiel smiled, raised his hands, and shrugged his shoulders. "How could I deny it? You know my handwriting. You know the parchment was stained to make it look old, like the scrolls of the Sacred House. You found the proof in my own workroom. How could I conceal from you the truth?"

Zadok was shaken by the priest's lack of concern at admitting the fraud. "But why? Why did you lie to us? Why did you claim divine authority for the *mishkan* when it was all your idea? The people believed in the scroll, and they believed in you. You have deceived them."

Ezekiel spoke softly. "Look around you, my son. Look at what you have accomplished for our people. Is all of this so bad? No. Our people are alive again." He smiled paternally at Zadok. "What makes you so certain this is not the plan of the Eternal One? This *mishkan* is a divine inspiration. How else would I have conceived this idea if God had not given it to me? It is not a lie. It works because God willed it. You should be proud of the part you have played."

Zadok sat down heavily on a stool. "How can I face our people, knowing the truth?"

"Do you think you know the truth? What is the truth? The truth is what our people believe to be true. They believe the *Mishkan Scroll* is real. It was your assurances that convinced them it was real. Besides, all we have now are copies of the scroll. The original scroll was destroyed in the fire."

"Was that a fraud as well?"

"The fire was real. Its destructive power was real."

"And very convenient."

Ezekiel grasped Zadok's face firmly in his hands and looked deeply into his eyes. "Now, Zadok, my son, you must make the same choices I made. Was I willing to do whatever it would take to ensure the survival of our people and our faith? My answer was yes. It is still yes today." He aimed his eyes at Zadok. "What is your answer? Tell me now."

Zadok's voice shook. This was the most difficult decision he ever made. Much was at stake. "I see now that you are doing the work of the Eternal. Yes, my master, for the sake of our people, I will say no more about the *Mishkan Scroll*."

Ezekiel moved his hands to Zadok's shoulders. "Do you so swear?"

Almost in a whisper, Zadok responded, "I swear."

Despite Zadok's solemn oath, Ezekiel knew in that moment that Zadok would not keep the secret of the true origins of the *Mishkan Scroll* secret for long. He may already have shared the truth with Miryam. The priest knew what had to be done. The question was when?

***

On the twenty-fourth day of the sixth month, the month the Bavlim call *Elul*, the barges transporting the *Mishkan* arrived at the landing near Pumbedita. Ezekiel decided that the Judean community would join the Bavlim in a celebration of the reign of their king. In keeping with ancient Bavli tradition, each year, at the beginning of the seventh month, a massive national celebration would symbolically renew the reign of the king for another year. From the day they arrived in Bavel, Judean exiles were welcome at the Temples of Ishtar and Marduk and invited to join in the celebration that featured much drinking of wine, beer, and the consumption of endless delicacies. Ezekiel was committed to weaning the Judeans away from the pagan temples by providing them with celebrations of their own, centered around the *mishkan*.

Coincident with the building of the *mishkan*, Pumbedita was becoming the largest center of Judean life in Bavel. That was why Ezekiel had the *mishkan* return to the site of its consecration. The anticipated crowds would impress the Bavli officials in attendance. Ezekiel believed that demonstrations of Judean loyalty to the Bavli king would be rewarded with a further lifting of certain restrictions placed upon the exiles when they arrived. Most of those restrictions were daily reminders of their exile status, such as rules limiting the number of Judeans gathered at one time in one place, or rules on their freedom of travel in Bavel. One prohibition, however, did stand out. Judeans were not permitted to bear arms. Ezekiel wanted to change that restriction. He knew that his only opportunity to do so would be when the Bavlim were convinced of Judean loyalty. Honoring the king at the *mishkan* would be a powerful sign of that growing loyalty. When the time was ripe, Ezekiel would petition the king to allow the Judeans to return to their home as a proven, loyal, military garrison, protecting the empire's western flank. He conjectured that Judeans serving in the army of the Bavlim would reflect well on all Judeans. The return to their homeland would be earned by the blood of Judean sons serving the king.

Having managed the set-up of the *mishkan* on many previous occasions, the Levites of the second watch were becoming adept at its assembly. The pieces came together a bit faster each month. With two days to go before the New Year of the King celebration, the *mishkan* was standing and ready.

At dinner, the night before the ceremony, Zadok was in a festive mood. Miryam prepared a number of vegetable dishes and ground beans with olive oil for dipping.

"Your feast was exceptional, as always," Zadok said.

"Stop with the false compliments. The only thing exceptional about the meal was the amount you consumed. What is it you desire, my husband?" Miryam placed her arms around his waist

"You know me so well. I desire to lie down and take a nap."

"I have a better idea. You have been cooped up inside and bent over your table for most of the day. Go take a walk. The evening air is cool and fresh. It will revive you."

"Revive me for what?"

Miryam smiled.

"I think I will obey my wife and go and check on the *mishkan*."

Zadok looked at the scene by the river as if for the first time. It was impressive. Fifteen cubits from the walls and twenty cubits apart, a series of basin lamps circled the compound. Filled with olive oil and a large wick, each lamp cast dancing shadows on the *mishkan*. Looking at the star-filled sky, Zadok was impressed at how the *mishkan* appeared to be an organic part of the landscape, as if it were meant to be there, on the banks of the river. *Perhaps the God of our ancestors truly did inspire Mar Ezekiel with a vision of this sacred place*, he thought.

Third Watch Levites patrolled the outer wall in pairs. Their distinctive garb made them easy to recognize. White robes with light blue sashes around their waists and white turbans on their heads set them apart from the other Judeans, out for an evening stroll.

***

When the High Priest appeared at her door, Miryam knew something was very wrong. "Mar Ezekiel, where is Zadok?"

"Miryam, I have some terrible news..."

Before he could complete his sentence, Miryam collapsed in a heap on the floor inside the doorway.

Ezekiel lifted Miryam into his arms and carried her to a bed in a connecting room. Miryam opened her eyes and saw Ezekiel standing over her. "What happened?" She managed to ask, fighting tears welling in her eyes.

Ezekiel held her hand. "A fisherman found Zadok's body snagged on a log, at the edge of the river. It was about half a *parasang* from the landing where the *mishkan* was assembled. Third watch Levites said they saw him walking around the perimeter of the *mishkan*, but they neither saw nor heard anything after that. The Levites ordered the fishermen to bring Zadok's body to my house."

"Do you know how it happened?" Miryam spoke as tears fell from her eyes.

"He must have stumbled in the dark and fallen into the river. There is a deep wound to the left side of his head. I asked the Levites to wash and prepare his body for burial. We shall bury him tomorrow. Come with me to my house. You should be with him."

Suddenly, as if the implications of Ezekiel's story had just broken through the haze of grief, Miryam exclaimed, "My lord, High Priest, how could you allow yourself to be in contact with a corpse? The rules of the *cohanim* prohibit contact with corpses except close family members. You will be unable to perform your duties for a week."

"He is not a corpse, Miryam. He's like a son to me. I cannot stay away."

Looking into the High Priest's eyes, Miryam came to a decision. "Please have Zadok brought back here. We shall watch over him until the burial. You have done more than enough."

Was her tone harsh? Ezekiel looked closely at Miryam. "I shall do as you have requested."

Miryam wondered why Ezekiel's eyes appeared to lose their warmth.

An hour later, after Zadok's body was removed from the home of the High Priest, and returned to his family, Ezekiel had visitors.

Shadows produced by the single, small oil lamp danced on the freshly plastered walls of Ezekiel's house. Evidence of the fire had all but disappeared and the rebuilt structure was more luxurious than even its predecessor. It was a home befitting the high priest and prophet tasked by God to rebuild his own home.

Ezekiel and his visitors, two Bavli rivermen, sat in his study, around a small table in the center of the room. The priest seldom met with Bavlim, certainly not after sunset. But his business with these men was urgent and he did not want them seen. He lowered his voice. "Did he suffer?"

One of the men shook his head. "No, my lord. One hard, swift blow was all it took."

The other held out his palm. "He was dead in an instant. As you commanded. Pay us and we will be gone."

Ezekiel wished the pain in his heart would also be gone.

In her house, Miryam leaned over the clay basin and gazed into the water. She stared at her eyes, red with tears and swollen. She splashed water on her face, then grabbed the edge of her tunic and ripped it down the side. She turned to look at her husband's body, lifeless on a table that witnessed countless meals and celebrations. She then cried out, "Blessed be the true Judge."

Preparing Zadok for burial was no easy task. His wet clothing still bore the smell of the river. Miryam began by untying the drawstring of his tunic. As she did so, she remembered a small pocket she had sewn into it, when she made it for Zadok. Slowly, she ran her fingers along the top edge, feeling for the pocket opening. It was there as she remembered it. There was something inside. She was surprised to find a folded sheet of papyrus, which she withdrew with great care.

Unfolding the document, Miryam stared at Zadok's corpse. "What is this?" She quickly realized that it was a letter written by Zadok and addressed to his brother, Eli, in Shomron. She sat down and read the letter and quickly hid it in her robe. "You knew, my dear husband. You knew." She bent over Zadok and kissed his lips. "You did not tell me to protect our children." She rose, her hands in tight fists. "Zadok, my dear, Mar Ezekiel may have killed you, but your brother shall have this letter. I swear this oath to the God of our ancestors, even if I must die, your brother shall know the truth."

CHAPTER FIFTEEN

DATE: March 18, 2009
TIME: 12:30 P.M. Local Time
PLACE: Holon, Israel

On a quiet street in Holon, a suburb of Tel Aviv, Professor Daniel Carlson was seated in his Peugeot. He looked into the mirror behind the driver-side visor. His face was heavily marked by abrasions and cuts from the bombing in Or Yehudah. This face would frighten both children and adults, he thought, as he gingerly dabbed at the painful sores with an antiseptic pad, wincing with each burning touch. Shouting in rhythm with each dab seemed to help. "Jesus H. Christ! God that hurts! Good Samaritans my ass!"

It was fortunate that Carlson left the windows up. He was, at that moment, sitting in the middle of the largest concentration of Samaritans in Israel. With the windows open, his shouts would have been heard all the way to Tel Aviv. He tossed the used pad onto the trash-strewn floor of his car, and then checked the last screen on his GPS device. Having satisfied himself that he had arrived close to his destination, he shut off the engine.

Carlson was in this section of Holon to attend an urgent meeting with the young Samaritan militants responsible for the wounds on his face. The five-building apartment block he was seeking was utilitarian and beige, a multi-story urban Samaritan village. The only real color in the neighborhood was provided by flapping laundry suspended on clotheslines from each apartment balcony.

Carlson carefully watched the arched entryway to the apartment block and noted that no one entered or left the complex without being screened by an always present band of young Samaritans. In a phone call setting up the meeting, Carlson was warned by his host that Samaritans were zealous about their privacy. The street numbers on each building had been lost or stolen forty years ago. The Samaritans reasoned that if you were a part of their community, you already knew where you were going. Carlson knew that without help from residents it would be impossible to locate a specific apartment. The only question now was how to ask for help? He need not have concerned himself. His arrival in the neighborhood did not go unnoticed. With his eyes focused on the apartment block across the street, Carlson failed to see the sudden appearance of four burly young men at the rear of the Peugeot. They began to pound mercilessly on the car until a commanding voice called a halt.

"Enough! Go back home. He is a guest of mine. I'll vouch for him."

Carlson's savior emerged from the apartment block. He was of medium height, trim build, and very dark complexion. His close-cropped hair was salt and pepper, mostly grey. His deep-set eyes were a transparent coffee color. He wore a t-shirt the color of his hair and a pair of olive-green slacks. Open sandals were on his feet. His orders to the young toughs were barked in Hebrew, but there was some other kind of accent that indicated Hebrew was not his native tongue.

"I am Tovya. Please forgive our young people. They do not observe the usual courtesies in the presence of strangers."

Carlson smiled stiffly. "Thank you for your timely arrival."

"Just so you know Professor, your presence was made known to me the moment you left the highway. We are not the only ones who watch the comings and goings of strangers. Follow me! We must go inside quickly."

Tovya led Carlson across the street and into an open stairwell of one of the apartment buildings set into the side of a hill. He started down the terrazzo paved stairs and continued for two flights below the level of the street. Four doors were on this lowest level, indicating four apartments. Carlson followed Tovya through the first door. All four apartments on this level were joined into one spacious, well-appointed, dwelling.

As if by some sort of magic, the same four burly young men who had rocked his car, were now inside to greet Carlson with a menacing display of thin smiles and folded muscular arms.

Carlson saw that a corner of the apartment faced the street and was furnished as an office behind a window wall, with a set of French doors closing it off from the rest of the room. Built-in bookshelves occupied the two walls that met in the corner with a desk built into the center. A small burgundy leather couch was against the wall with the door in it, the one opposite the desk. Tovya motioned to Carlson to take a seat on the couch. He sat across from him in a black desk chair.

"Would you care for something to drink?" Toyva asked.

"As a matter of fact, I would."

Tovya nodded his head ever so slightly to one of the burly boys who was standing just outside the office area. A few moments later he returned, carrying a brass tray, and set it down on the desk. An antique brass teapot with a long, graceful spout, was flanked by two ceramic mugs, bearing the logo of the Maccabee Tel Aviv basketball team. Sugar packets and small containers of cream were scattered around the tray. A red packet of almond cookies, saved from some airline, completed the presentation. Tovya motioned to Carlson to help himself.

When Carlson settled back on the couch, Tovya poured himself some tea, added some cream, and opened the conversation. "It is important to me that you understand why we are willing to partner with you and go to such extreme lengths to obtain the Ezra Scroll, even so far as to take lives in the process."

"The scroll will be yours for the agreed upon price. I personally am not interested in how you justify your actions."

Tovya continued as if he had not heard Carlson at all. "We believe that God allows us to take a life, only when the very survival of our people is in jeopardy. The Ezra Scroll in the wrong hands is just such a threat."

Carlson set his cup down and looked directly at Tovya. "You are not very good at the targeting part, are you?"

"We were devastated to learn that our bomb destroyed an innocent family. In this part of the world, Israelis and Palestinians, with all of their wars, have more experience than we do at making things blow up."

Carlson's anger overcame his fear of the burly boys. He shouted, "Are you that incompetent? You nearly killed me! I am still picking glass out of my face and scalp."

With a quiet voice Tovya responded. "You were not standing where I told you to stand." Tovya held his hands out in a placating gesture. "May you enjoy a complete healing from your wounds."

"Enough with the excuses. We became partners to possess the scroll. You will pay me handsomely for the original scroll. How you take care of any copies and the people now racing to decipher its meaning, is your business."

Tovya pointed toward the top of the desk. "Let's get down to the business at hand. You have in your possession the original text. Yes?"

"Let's just say it's in a safe place. And before you ask, yes, I stole it for the money. My price for the scroll will be an amount that will guarantee a very comfortable retirement for me and my wife."

Tovya nodded his head. "Of course, that is how it should be, my friend."

Carlson continued. "And while I am on the subject, my wife has already left Israel for our new retirement location. You will not be able to kidnap her to use her as leverage. You will get the scroll upon payment confirmation. You know the transaction details. Your failure to destroy the copies of the scroll means that someone else will be able to discover their meaning and profit from it."

Tovya put his cup down and sat on the edge of his seat. "Perhaps then, we should not concern ourselves with copies. What can you tell me about the scroll itself? Why are you so sure that it is an ancient Samaritan text?"

Carlson was eager to finish the meeting and confirm that payment was received but found comfort in entering teaching mode. "For starters, you must understand that the scroll is truly priceless, regardless of what it might or might not reveal. Each of the usual tests confirm it is written on parchment prepared in the time of Ezra, around 450 BCE, plus or minus twenty years. The scroll, therefore, is at least four hundred years older than the oldest texts of the Dead Sea Scrolls. That fact alone makes it an extraordinary find."

Tovya's voice started to rise. "But is it a Samaritan text?"

Carlson gently stroked the wounds on his face. "As I explained in my email, it is a carefully crafted version of Psalm 137. Line-for-line, it is nearly identical to the oldest known written version of that psalm found in the Aleppo Codex, from thirteen hundred years later. The lettering is also consistent with the 450 BCE date, but with an interesting twist."

"And what is that?" Tovya asked.

"It was the style of the Hebrew letters. That is what prompted me to contact you in the first place. The lettering is consistent with Samaritan language inscriptions of the period and not Hebrew ones."

"So, what is the problem with that?"

"Babylonian Jews of that period used Aramaic style letters, not Samaritan style. Therefore, we need to answer this question. What is a Samaritan copy of Psalm 137, a psalm with a clear connection to the exiles of Judah, doing in Babylonia? Modern research of this period assumes a great deal of enmity existed between Jews and Samaritans."

"So?" Tovya said.

"The Marine and my former student, Rabbi Stone, claim the scroll was discovered in a *genizah* in Fallujah. If this is true, it would mean a scroll produced by a Samaritan scribe was preserved by the Jewish community in Babylonia." He looked at Tovya. "It means we do not know as much about ancient Jews and Samaritans as we thought we did." He glanced at his watch, eager to end this lesson. "Even if we cannot answer all the questions, this scroll is proof that meaningful contacts existed between the Samaritans and the Jews from the very beginning of the Judean exile."

Tovya smiled. "I have been expecting this news."

"You have?"

"In fact, this information confirms one of our oldest Samaritan traditions."

"And that would be?"

"That a Samaritan leader was in contact with the Jews of Babylonia around the time of Ezra.

"Is that it? Just contact?" Asked Carlson.

"Look, forget stories of enmity between Samaritans and Judeans. This Samaritan lettered scroll apparently contains a message. Someone, Judean or Samaritan, is trying to communicate with Judeans, but using Samaritan letters. Why?"

Carlson considered likely reasons. "Whoever the author of the scroll is, he does not want all Judeans in Babylon to be able to read it."

Tovya smiled broadly. "Indeed! One possible answer is found in that ancient Samaritan tradition I mentioned earlier. Let me quote my sainted grandfather. 'Behold, from Mount Gerizim in Samaria the Torah will go forth.' He was citing ancient traditions handed down from one Samaritan generation to the next. The Torah originated in Samaria!"

Carlson shook his head. "That's a misquote from Isaiah, Chapter 2 verse 3. *For Torah will go forth from Zion.*

"Dear professor, why should you be any different than the rest of the so-called Judeo-Christian world? The very idea of Samaritan authorship of the Torah has been denounced and ridiculed down through the ages. The single most disputed part of that tradition is the one that holds that the actual Torah belonged to Samaritans first. It was our scribes who brought it together. Our scribes made it known to our people and so, perhaps, one of our scribes was sending a copy of that Torah to the Jews in Babylonia."

"The majority of Bible scholars claim that the first time Samaritans encountered the Torah was during the period of the Hasmoneans, you know, the Maccabees, about four hundred years later. "

"Do you agree with that, Professor?" Tovya asked.

"Until now, I did. The consensus theory among those scholars was that, as enmity grew between the Samaritans and the Maccabees, Samaritan priests altered the original text, replacing Zion with Mount Gerizim in Samaria, as God's chosen mountain. Now I have my doubts."

"Thank you for your willingness to keep an open mind."

Carlson looked thoughtful. "So, this scroll is important because it may prove that the Torah was originally produced by the Samaritans and later falsely claimed by the Jews as their own?" He let out a silent whistle as the impact of the discovery hit him.

"Indeed, it just might."

"Well, which is it? Was it adopted by the Jews, given to the Jews, or stolen by the Jews?"

"That is the mystery we Samaritans hope the newly discovered scroll will solve. Now, perhaps you will understand, Professor, why it is so important that we decipher this text. What it contains may lift my people from the dung heap of history. Instead of being the unwanted backward stepchild of Judaism and Christianity, we Samaritans will possess proof that our ancestors are the authors of the one text that inspires all of Western religious tradition. Without a Samaritan connection, there would be no Hebrew Scriptures, no New Testament, no Koran."

Carlson narrowed his eyes and was wary. "You said that your tradition allows the taking of human life if your community is threatened. How does this scroll's discovery threaten your community? If the scroll disappears today, nothing changes. The status quo remains."

Tovya's jaw tightened. "For my people, the status quo means our extinction. Our numbers are so small that in recent years our priests have given permission for our men to marry Jewish women, so long as they adopt our religion. We, the last Samaritans, are living artifacts, known only to a few dedicated scholars." He leaned closer. "International assistance programs pass us by. We are trapped between the 'rock' of Israel, and the 'hard place' of Palestine. We barely exist."

Carlson did not feel sorry for the anguish of the Samaritan. He wondered when his host would allow him to leave.

Tovya wanted Carlson to understand why the scroll was significant enough that he would murder for it. "You must understand that for other than those few scholars who wish to preserve us like some specimen in a petri dish, and study us under their micro-scope, we are seen as an inconvenience. The Israelis complain we receive too much welfare from them. The Palestinians covet our lands around Nablus." He shook his head. "We need to upset the status quo. It is killing us. Israeli politics have become totally dependent on placating the Black Hats, the Ultra-Orthodox. If the state-sponsored archeologists decipher the scroll, and realize how it threatens their beliefs, they will bury it in some obscure vault never to be seen again. Trust me. They do not wish to incur the wrath of their rabbis."

Carlson was skeptical. "But the Israeli government is not involved in this scroll business. Are they?"

Tovya smiled. "How naïve you are, Professor. Do you imagine that after two failed attempts on the lives of the Americans, the Israeli security services have not become involved?" He held up two fingers. "As I see it, they have two problems. First, how to obtain the scroll copies from the Americans. Second, how to steal back the original scroll from you. When I get the scroll from you, my friend, it is no longer your worry. It will be my problem. All mine."

The young Samaritan who had brought in the brass tray knocked on the French doors. Tovya waved him in.

"This email just arrived from the Bank of the Cayman Islands," the young man said with a knowing smile on his face.

"Thank you, Amram," Tovya replied. He passed the paper to Carlson. "As you can see, the ten million Euros have been deposited into your island account. And now, if you do not mind, the location of the scroll. Please."

Carlson took his cell phone from his pocket and entered a few keystrokes. "Give me a moment so I can confirm the transaction. Anyone can send a convincing email." He studied the screen. "It is confirmed. Thank you so much." He glanced at the guards at the door and then turned back to Tovya. "You will find the scroll in the guest safe of room 502 of the Carlton Hotel, in Tel Aviv. When I am safely away from Holon, I will call you on your cell phone and give you the four-number code for the safe." He reached into his pocket. "Here are the keys to the room. I checked in using my own name. The room is mine until noon tomorrow."

Toyva examined the key. "Professor, if you betray me and my people in this matter, and do not call with that code within the hour, we shall track you down and kill you, your wife, and anyone else that is close to you."

"Tovya, you need not threaten me. I want you to have that scroll. I will make the call." He stood, praying the guards would not stop him from leaving.

***

The voices of Carlson and the Samaritan were crystal clear. Keller and Stone heard every word. So did Malik, Rafi and Omar. They were still in the conference room on the fourth floor of the department store in downtown Tel Aviv. Rafi and Omar did not bother to explain the means by which the listening devices had been planted on Carlson or the Samaritan, or on both. Keller assumed they had a Shin Bet agent working inside the *Keter Shomron* organization. He put nothing past the Israeli agents.

Stone stood and slammed an open hand on the table. "We need to get to that Hotel first and make sure the scroll lands in **our** hands."

Keller admired Stone's determination but wondered if Abby really understood how dangerous dealing with these Samaritans could be. His fingers tightened on the holster on his belt.

CHAPTER SIXTEEN

DATE: Second Day of the Twelfth Month, In the Forty-Sixth Year Since the Destruction of Jerusalem
TIME: First Hour of the Second Daylight Watch
PLACE: Pumbedita on the Eastern Bank of the River Frat

An unusually warm spring sun illuminated the scope of the flood's massive devastation. The once-thriving community of Judeans in Pumbedita was all but gone. Forty-six years earlier, the Bavlim purposely placed the Judean exiles at the edge of town in the flood plain. In the years that followed, annual floods were an expected annoyance, a challenge the exiles were resigned to face in their struggle to survive. Each time the annual floods struck, the Judeans coped as best they could, rebuilding with better designs and stronger materials. But not even fired brick could withstand the force of this year's flood. Was it any wonder that the sacred *mishkan* was also demolished and its beautiful furnishings were carried downstream?

It would be weeks before any of the survivors would speak about what happened to the *mishkan*. Not enough of the *cohanim* survived to organize the daily offering of sacrifices. Even if they had, there was no longer a sacred place to perform the rituals. Those Judeans still alive were overwhelmed by the grim task of gathering the corpses of family members and locating ground deemed high enough for proper burial. Once the numbness of the tragedy faded, many looked for someone, or something, to blame. Some suggested the *mishkan* was destroyed because God was angry with the Judeans for offering sacrifices outside of Jerusalem.

Four-year-old Hilkiah stood in silence, watching his grandmother weep. He was too young to comprehend what they had lost. He just needed to be close to his *savta*. He walked to her side and gripped her left hand tightly. Together they looked out at the raging river. Aunts, uncles, cousins, were all gone. Hilkiah's father, Shallum, his mother,

Aviva, and his baby brother, Chayim Ariel, were among the hundreds who disappeared from their community when the torrent of water escaped the banks of the Euphrates and smashed through Pumbedita. Hilkiah, and his grandmother, Miryam, widow of Zadok the scribe, were the only members of their immediate family still alive.

Miryam demonstrated a fierce determination to overcome the infirmity of her age. Only two days after the floodwaters receded, the bodies of her dear ones were found entangled in the roots of a willow tree. At that terrible moment, she vowed to take no rest until Shallum, Aviva and Chayim Ariel had a proper burial.

Miryam marked off a burial space on high ground and began to dig with her bare hands. Little Hilkiah, seeing his grandmother working so hard, picked up stones and broken mud bricks and tossed them out of the hole. Together, they managed to finish digging the grave an hour before sunset.

Miryam stood at the edge and gazed into the clay-walled grave. She looked into Hilkiah's dark eyes and smiled. "You did well, my grandson, but there is no time to rest. We must finish before dark." She did what she could to prepare the bodies. With rags rinsed in nearby standing pools of flood waters, Miryam washed as much of the river mud from the bodies as her fading strength would allow. She wrapped each corpse in shrouds made from whatever scraps of cloth she could scavenge from the riverbank. When she finished her preparations, she realized that no one was nearby to help her place the bodies into the ground.

Weeping from grief and frustration and completely exhausted, she pushed the corpses gently over the edge and into the grave.

Hilkiah watched his grandmother intently, not understanding the enormity of the tragedy.

The corpses made an awful sound when they landed at the bottom of the pit. Miryam felt the sound as if it was coursing through her body. That thought made her physically ill.

"Blessed be God, the true Judge," Miryam whispered. She looked at Hilkiah and took a deep breath. "Let us finish. Help me push the soil into the grave."

"Won't the soil hurt them?" Hilkiah asked.

"They cannot feel the soil, my precious grandson. It will be like a warm blanket for them."

"If they cannot feel the soil, how will they feel the warm blanket?"

Miryam smiled lovingly at her grandson. "You are wise beyond your years. The truth is these bodies are only empty containers. That which made them your father, your mother, and your little brother is no longer within them. The breath of God that gives all things life has returned to the Eternal One who gave it to them."

"Are they with God?"

"Yes."

The questions ended and the sad work continued. An hour later, with stones covering the mound of earth over the grave, Miryam stood and gazed beyond the graveyard to the mud-brown waters of the Euphrates. The waters had taken so much from her. "Hilkiah, we are done here," she said.

"Can we come back and visit them?"

"They are not here." With tears welling in her eyes, Miryam picked Hilkiah up into her arms and carried him down the hill, back to the mounds of debris deposited by the swollen river.

In the jumbled mess of the debris field, Miryam observed well-dressed, well-fed, Bavli officials swarming over the area. Shaking with rage she shouted, "Why are you here? Does the destruction of Judeans amuse you? Help us!"

Hilkiah began to cry at his *savta's* outburst.

Miryam set him down, gently. "It is okay, dear child," she said, still glaring at the scavenging officials.

A *cohein,* wearing a mud-spattered turban and a flimsy tunic, quickly approached Miryam. He placed his hand on her shoulder.

Miryam was surprised to see it was Yeshuah, Ezekiel's former assistant.

Yeshuah whispered, "Miryam, they are not worth it. They don't care about Judeans. Now is not the time to antagonize them." He nodded toward Hilkiah. "Think about the little one."

Miryam focused on Yeshuah, then turned to pick Hilkiah up. "You are right. They don't care about us, just our taxes."

Lifting two small children of his own into his arms, Yeshuah wiped away their tears. "Now, they are the only thing that matters around here, not property nor money. We need to be strong for them."

Miryam was surprised. Yeshuah was not the doddering fool she had believed him to be. What he said was practical. He was a realist. "You are right," she said. "My grandson is what matters to me now." She hugged Hilkiah and offered a silent thank you to God for sparing him.

It was sunset, the end of the second day since the flood subsided. In the fading light, Judean survivors shouted curses at one another, as they scoured the riverbank to salvage anything of value. Unfortunately, the extreme conditions that followed in the wake of the flood left many Judeans more desperate than rational.

Miryam did her own share of pushing and grabbing. Having spent the first night of the flood sleeping on water-soaked ground, she was determined to provide Hilkiah with shelter for this night. Just before stars were visible in the sky, she began her search for something she might use for a tent. She made her way slowly down to the water's edge, but she nearly slid into the still-raging river. A piece of heavy cloth, nearly six cubits square, had been snagged on a scruffy-looking willow. She grasped at the cloth to stop her slide. The cloth and willow held firm and she pulled herself up the slippery bank.

Hilkiah watched as his grandmother untangled the cloth and stuffed it into her nearly shredded cloak. She climbed back up the riverbank, smothered Hilkiah in a hug, then sat down hard. The two survivors sat motionless until Miryam caught her breath, stood, and grasped Hilkiah by the hand. They started to walk, following other survivors making their way to higher ground. In the distance, away from the river to the east, Miryam saw the flickering flames of a dozen or so fires. There were more survivors. As she and Hilkiah drew closer to the fires, the sound of voices carried toward them. Perhaps here, she would find help.

"Sit down, sister, and rest. Who is this good-looking lad that holds your hand so tightly?" The invitation came from a woman who could have been a grandmother herself. She was dressed in a brown mud-spattered tunic that did not fit her well. She poked a thin stick at a small fire to stir the embers.

Miryam cleared her throat. "He is my grandson, Hilkiah. The last of our family."

"You don't have to explain it to me." The woman nodded sadly. "Mine too are all gone. I am Yocheved, widow of Shimshon, bereft mother of Talia. Come close to the fire and dry yourself and the little one."

Miryam did as instructed. Then she looked beyond Yocheved's fire and saw the others. Each small fire was surrounded by groups of survivors in various states of disarray.

"None of them have any food." Yocheved anticipated Miryam's question. "There is a rumor going around that the Bavli are collecting food for us. First, they take our food in taxes, and then they give it back to us."

"Why should they help Judeans?" Miryam asked.

Yocheved threw a block of pressed camel dung on the fire. Sparks flew into the air. "Perhaps the Bavli fear that starving people are dangerous."

Miryam withdrew from her cloak the cloth she had pulled from the river and spread it on the ground before the fire. She stared at the square fabric, seeing its design for the first time. The caked mud obscured the pattern, but the outlines of the Lions of Judah were still visible. "How fitting. The wife and grandson of Zadok, the murdered scribe, will be sheltered under a panel from the destroyed *mishkan*."

Yocheved looked up from the fire. "What's that you say?"

"Praised be the God of our ancestors, the protector of widows and orphans," Miryam whispered.

Hilkiah let out a tiny whimper.

"He is starved, the poor child," Miryam said.

"I am afraid we must all become accustomed to hunger and deprivation," Yocheved said.

Miryam shook her head, a determined expression on her face. "I will not let anything hurt this child, even if I must give my life to God to save him." As Miryam looked at Hilkiah, her mind recalled a conversation she had with her first-born son, Shallum, fifteen years ago.

On the day Shallum became thirteen years of age, he was formally bound to the observance of God's commandments by the *cohanim*, in a community celebration which took place before the entrance to the *mishkan*. When the ceremony concluded, Miryam embraced Shallum, kissed him, and invited him to walk with her away from the *mishkan*. She told him she needed to have a private word with him. If Shallum was old enough to be obligated to God, Miryam reasoned, then he was now old enough to know his father had been murdered at the command of Ezekiel, the High Priest. She revealed the same terrible secret to her second son, Reuven, when he became *bar mitzvah*, old enough to be obligated to the commandments. Trying to make sense of their mother's awful revelation, their questions were nearly identical. "How can the High Priest get away with murder? Isn't it a crime to kill and lie in the name of God? Miryam's response was sharp and terse. "Yes, they are indeed crimes. And no, he won't get away with them." Whenever Ezekiel's name was mentioned in her presence, she spat and uttered a simple curse, "May his name be erased from under the heavens." She could not let go of her grief and bitterness. Despite its daily importance in the lives of the Judeans, Miryam taught her sons to despise t he *mishkan* and all it stood for. She impressed upon them that it was a fraud built on murder and lies. She made sure that they understood their father Zadok was murdered solely to keep him from exposing the forgery of the *mishkan scroll*.

Back then, Miryam consoled herself with her conviction that Zadok's murder was a crime that God would not forgive. *There will be a reckoning and accounting of this blasphemy. God's justice will occur in God's time, not ours.*

***

Staring into Yocheved's fire, Miryam spoke to the embers. "Well, my precious husband, I guess God's justice is swifter than I would have expected,"

"*Savta*, grandmother, who are you talking to?" Hilkiah asked half-asleep.

"I am talking to your grandfather."

"But he is dead. Can he hear you?" Hilkiah asked.

"Yes. All our beloved dead can hear us. We speak with those we love who are no longer living when we are troubled, unsure of what we should do. They are always with us."

"So true, so true," Yocheved muttered.

"Are you troubled now, *savta?*"

Miryam smiled sadly. "I miss them all so much."

Hilkiah once again grasped his grandmother's hand. "I know what we should do next. We should make a tent. I am tired. We should sleep."

Was it simply childhood innocence that caused Hilkiah to change the subject, or was he trying to offer comfort to his grief-stricken grandmother? Miryam was not sure, but she welcomed the opportunity to do something with her grandson that might distract her from dark thoughts "Hilkiah, I hear the wisdom of your mother in your words. That is exactly what we shall do."

For the next hour, in the dim light of Yocheved's fire, Miryam and Hilkiah fumbled with the waterlogged cloth and random strands of braided reeds until they raised a tent. She helped Hilkiah to find a spot close to the front opening and tucked him in. She covered his thin body with her goat hair cloak. When she heard his rhythmic breathing, thinking Hilkiah was asleep, she called to her new friend, "Yocheved, there is room for you in our tent. Come join us."

Yocheved smiled. "I will sit here and keep the fire going. I need to get all the warmth I can. You and the little one need rest. At dawn, you can tend the fire and I shall sleep."

"Why does the sky glow orange, *savta*?" Hilkiah's question caught Miryam by surprise. She looked at the sky toward the east. "It usually means there is a large fire burning."

"Larger than our fire? Will the fire burn us?"

Miryam peered at the smoke and flame in the distance. "No. Of course not. The glow means the fire is far away from us. I will never let anything hurt you. Now, close your eyes, turn over, and let sleep overtake you."

Miryam knew from the distance and direction, that a large fire was burning in the area occupied by the government of the Bavlim. She was too physically and emotionally drained to care about what it meant. She and her grandson had nothing more to lose. For the time being, they were safe.

That night, Miryam slept fitfully, unable to find a position that would not add more pain to her aching body. She was grateful Hilkiah slept soundly.

At dawn, their new guardian, Yocheved, pushed aside the flap on their makeshift tent. She signaled to Miryam that she would exchange places with her and try to get some rest. They managed to change places without waking Hilkiah. Miryam tended the fire.

In late morning, with the sun bright and warm, Hilkiah emerged from the tent and ran to his grandmother's side. He rubbed sleep from his eyes and drowsily asked. "*Savta,* what are you doing?"

Miryam replied, "Hilkiah, I am trying to keep this fire going. We need some wood or dry reeds for the fire. Look carefully on the ground and walk in a circle, always keeping me in view. Do you understand?"

"Yes, *savta,* but when can we eat?"

"Soon, little one, soon," Miryam replied without much conviction. "Go search for straw and wood." Poking a long stick into the fire and stirring the embers, Miryam was finding hope to be in as short supply as kindling.

The braying of an ass caused Miryam to turn her head to the west.

It was Yeshuah, the *cohein,* riding toward her. As she observed his progress, she noted that at least he had found some more clothing with which to cover himself.

Yeshuah dismounted and held the ass by a thin leather lead. He looked curiously at Miryam's tent and then frowned. "I cannot believe that you have made a tent from the sacred cloth of the *mishkan.* That is sacrilege, woman!"

Miryam glared at Yeshuah in disbelief. "Our people have been decimated by a flood. Their surviving children are crying for food, and this is what you trouble me about? Haven't you heard? There is no sacred *mishkan.* Why are you here?"

Yeshuah turned toward the ass and rummaged around in a cloth saddlebag, withdrawing a hand-sized piece of bread. "This is for you and your grandson."

Miryam's eyes narrowed in shock and surprise. "Thank you for remembering us. Can you spare any more? The grandmother that helped us, Yocheved, is sleeping in the tent. She is as desperate as we are."

Yeshuah peered at the tent again and then shook his head. "You must share yours with her. This is all I have been able to find." He lowered his voice. "We are all in a bad way. Most of our *cohanim* perished in the flood." He sighed. "I will keep searching for food."

Miryam motioned for Hilkiah, still circling the area just beyond the campfire, to halt his search for straw and come to her. She broke off a small portion of the bread and gave it to him. She watched him eat as she spoke to the *cohein*. "There are rumors that the Bavli will feed us."

"They are gone," Yeshuah said.

It took a moment for Miryam to make sense of Yeshuah 's statement. "What do you mean, 'gone?'"

"The armies of the Medes and Persians are now in charge. They took command of the Royal Palace last night. That was the glow from the palace fires we saw in the dark."

"The Bavli are gone," Miriam repeated, trying to digest this news.

Yeshua nodded. "Our few surviving elders and I have orders to assemble whatever leadership of our people remains alive, to meet with the new rulers this afternoon."

"So why do you come to me?" Miryam suspected Yeshuah had not just appeared to provide bread for Zadok's widow.

Yeshuah sighed. "You are as astute as ever. We shall have need of a skilled scribe. The Persians insist that a careful record be made of the meeting between them and our people. It is fortunate that Zadok, may his memory be for a blessing, saw fit to train you. It appears that you are the only surviving scribe among us."

Miryam looked Yeshuah in the eye. "Are the Persians ordering us or inviting us?"

The priest nodded in the direction of Hilkiah. "Miryam, it is both. If you care for the future of your grandson, you will attend the meeting with your writing materials."

Miryam held her palms up. "I have no such materials. I have my grandson, the clothes on my back...and the tent of which you wish to deprive Zadok's grandson."

Yeshuah looked angry but calmed himself. "Then we shall do what we can to find some cold embers and papyrus for you." He stiffened. "The meeting will take place in three hours, down near the landing. Already there are rumors that the emperor's barge will be docking there for this event."

"Do you believe the Persians will be more willing to help us survive than the Bavli?"

"I guess you will have to judge for yourself." Yeshuah walked toward his mount. "For the sake of your grandson, be there," he said and rode away.

"For the sake of my grandson, and the memory of the rest of our family, I will be there," Miryam said, wondering what the new rulers had in mind for the long-suffering Judeans.

Miryam placed Hilkiah in the able care of Yocheved, who made a game of salvaging useful materials from the ample flood debris all around them. Knowing her grandson was safe, for the moment, she prepared for the meeting with the Persians. She walked down to the river, found a secluded spot, and bathed herself as best she could. She started with her filthy clothes on, so she could wash them as well. Then she stripped and immersed herself in the waters, holding on to an overhanging tree branch so she would not be swept away. She prayed that the wet clothing would dry in the bright sunlight in the time for the meeting.

As Miryam approached the river landing on the footpath, she observed that the Judean leadership gathering there was anything but impressive. She wondered how these elders were selected. She felt uncomfortable being the only woman among them.

Some of the men stared at Miryam but none openly challenged her presence.

Yeshuah soon arrived and introduced Miryam to the others as the widow of the great scribe, Zadok, and a talented scribe herself. He handed her a polished cedarwood container.

Miryam saw the box had a slanted top, copper-lined inkwell, and when opened, a compartment for parchment and papyrus.

While some of the newly commissioned elders understood Miryam's assigned task and were placated by Yeshuah's introduction, several muttered their disapproval.

When the Persian delegation arrived, the Judean leaders drew near to the landing, trying to catch a glimpse of the arrival of the new rulers. Miriam remained behind. The stench of some in the Judean assemblage made clear that she was among the few that took the time to bathe. What would the new rulers think of Judeans? She worried, wishing Zadok were with her.

Just then, the royal barge appeared around a bend in the river. It was about fifty cubits long. Made of a dark wood of a kind unfamiliar to Miryam, it gleamed in the midday sun like a cut jewel in a mirrored setting. Five strong oarsmen on each side of the vessel stood with oars raised at attention. A gigantic, dark-skinned helmsman worked the rudder back and forth, expertly guiding it to the rebuilt dock by the landing.

In a sky-blue robe that shimmered and reflected light from the sun, a tall, stern-looking man with shaved head and close-cropped beard stepped onto the dock and strode purposefully toward the Judeans.

The Judeans prostrated themselves on the muddy ground as a sign of submission to their new ruler.

A Persian next to the man in the shimmering robe came ashore. His eyes surveyed the Judeans with a look of authority. Then he declared in a loud voice, "Rise! This is the local governor, not your Emperor. But now you know that he speaks with the authority of our great ruler, Cyrus of Persia."

The man in the blue robe stepped up on a small platform set down for him by his second-in-command. In a commanding voice, he announced, "With our great victory over the Bavli, Cyrus, emperor of Medes and the great Persian Empire, has graciously appointed me as the Governor of Bavel. I will speak only with the leaders of the Judean community. The words of our great Emperor are for them and them alone."

Miryam saw Yeshuah bow his head. "Please, most Exalted Governor, come find shelter beneath our humble pavilion." She reasoned that as the oldest surviving *cohein*, Yeshua was chosen by the elders to speak on behalf of the community. She was not sure how she felt about that decision. He had never impressed her before.

Yeshuah extended his hand in the direction of a colorful canopy situated on higher ground about three hundred cubits from the landing. The covering was hastily erected that morning.

Miryam turned toward the pavilion and stared in disbelief. She struggled not to burst into laughter. The pattern on the canopy appeared familiar. She herself had supervised the weaving of this material for the *mishkan*. Now, that cloth was part of a patchwork of fabrics scavenged from the debris of the *mishkan*. She mused that she was not the only one who found a 'good,' if 'profane' use for the once sacred cloth.

Beneath the canopy, only one large wood seat was set on a small platform at the front. Behind the chair, off to one side, was a small writing table and wood chair. The Persian Governor was escorted by his bodyguards to the seat.

Cups and pitchers of watery beer were served to the dignitaries by several young boys, orphaned by the flood, now in the care of Zera, the wife of Yeshuah.

When Miryam learned of Yeshuah and his wife's act of compassion, her suspicions about Yeshuah softened. She allowed herself a slight smile to the priest when he motioned for her to be seated at the writing table behind the Persian governor.

None of the Judeans dared speak. They had no idea what to expect from their new rulers. Would they be as harsh as the Bavli overlords? Would they be better, or God forbid, worse? A few leaders took careful sips of the warm and slightly sweet beer, but their eyes never left the man on the platform.

The governor rose to speak. When he did, the people in the pavilion stood in absolute silence.

With a hint of a smile, the Governor extended his arms. "Judeans, thank you for your gracious welcome." He spoke to them in Aramaic, the language of the Bavlim and the language adopted by the Judeans. "People of Judah, from the Province beyond the River, I am Memukan, as of now, the governor of this province of the greater empire of Persia. I speak with the authority and seal of His Majesty, Cyrus." He grasped a cord around his neck and held it out to show an attached cylinder seal. Seated behind him, Miryam was making a valiant effort to transcribe his words. She wished he would speak slower.

With a sweeping gesture of his arms towards the landing, he continued. "The catastrophic flood wiped out almost all crops planted this winter for spring harvest. There will indeed be famine in this land. Our Emperor seeks ways to ensure that there will be enough food to get all our lands to the next planting and harvest. His Imperial Majesty, Cyrus of Media and Persia, has therefore decided to end your captivity. Your exile from Judah is at an end. You may return to the land of your ancestors."

It was the very loud, clear voice of the *cohein,* Yeshuah that broke through the stunned silence. "O Household of Israel, your redemption has begun!"

Miriam, stunned, dropped her stylus. How would this news impact their survival? Was she the only one contemplating the hard road ahead?

CHAPTER SEVENTEEN

DATE: March 18, 2009
TIME: 5:45 P.M. Local Time
PLACE: On the Beach Behind The Carlton Hotel, 10 Eliezer Peri Street, Tel Aviv

The sunset was like a religious painting from the Italian Renaissance. The contrast with the steel-gray Mediterranean was spectacular. Clouds from the west were perfectly aligned across the sun, producing long and wide beams of light radiating outward from above and below the formation. Tel Aviv is almost militantly secular, but this view had a definite spiritual quality about it. The tranquil beauty of the moment was about to be shattered.

Earlier in the day, the close surveillance of the Samaritan leader, Tovya, in Holon, by the Israeli Security Service, paid off handsomely. Professor Carlson's plan to exchange the *Ezra Scroll* for ransom at a Tel Aviv beachfront hotel was revealed early enough in the day to allow the Shin Bet to move quickly to get its operatives in position for the exchange. With the store owner's enthusiastic support, they established their command post in an ALDO ice cream parlor, behind the Carlton Hotel. The store was at the beginning of the *Tayelet,* the Tel Aviv Beach Promenade, a broad concrete walkway with swirling mosaic-like designs that framed the beach. From the Carlton Hotel, the walkway extended south nearly four kilometers to the outskirts of Jaffa.

Waiting out an anti-terror operation from an ice cream parlor was not in any Marine Corps manual Gunnery Sgt. Aaron Keller had studied. His nerves would not allow him to sit still. Rabbi Abby Stone, on the other hand, was passing the time licking a single dip of mint chocolate chip in a sugar cone. Even during his fidgeting, Keller found the image was sexy. Stone paused long enough to adopt a scolding tone of voice. "Sergeant, stop bouncing your legs, you will wear yourself out."

"I can't help it. I'm bored and anxious, and still mad that Rafi and Omar would not let me participate in the takedown. I found the damn scroll. I should be there to recover it. How can you calmly eat ice cream at a time like this?"

Stone dabbed at the corners of her mouth with a small napkin. "Rafi was polite enough to explain to us about Israeli liability laws should an innocent bystander get hurt in such an operation. More importantly, he pointed out the magnitude of probable fallout should an American Marine get hurt or killed. On the other hand, Omar did not even offer me the courtesy of a response. He just turned his back and left. It was like I didn't even exist."

Malik thought ice cream was a great mood enhancer. "You should try the pistachio, Sergeant. It is always excellent. You can tell a lot about a person by the way they eat an ice cream cone. Some like the long, slow, lick. Others bite into the ice cream with great violence. And then there are those who seek to prolong the experience by taking dainty licks like a kitten—"

"Do you mind, Professor, I am trying to concentrate here."

"Concentrate on what? There is nothing for us to do but wait patiently for the *Shin Bet* to retrieve our scroll. Have an ice cream, it will calm your nerves."

"My nerves are calm."

"Yes, I can see just how calm you are."

Stone shook her head slowly from side to side. "You two should take this show on the road. Let's just make sure that we do as Rafi ordered and keep our eyes on the beach-level service door to the hotel." She said all of this, never taking her eyes off the door.

A young man and a young woman sat on a small bench to the left side of the door. A full-sized baby carriage was between them. Posing as Israeli parents resting after a walk on the *Tayelet*, they were disguised *Shin Bet* operatives guarding the exit. From time to time, the man or the woman would lift their hand to their mouth and speak into the cuff of their sleeve. An occasional nod towards the window of the ice cream parlor was the only indication Abby received to indicate whether there was any progress in the operation.

Malik suddenly stood up and tossed his ice cream cone into the trash. "Shit! This is all wrong! Sergeant, use the radio and get them out of that hotel room. Now!"

Keller got to his feet and rushed to the window. "They never gave me a radio! What's the matter?"

"The ten million euros. That's what's the matter," Malik answered.

"Right. It was deposited in the numbered account. So?"

Stone asked the ten million Euro question. "Where did the Samaritans get the money? The Israel-based Samaritans in Holon are a modestly successful community, but they do not have the resources to wire transfer ten million euros around the world." Stone's eyes were still locked on the rear exit of the hotel.

Malik nodded. "Exactly my point. You are a very clever rabbi. You remind me of my teacher in Baghdad."

Stone smirked. "Your teacher in Baghdad had a chest-length beard and a lifestyle from the twelfth century. Where do you think they got the money, Professor?"

"From the Palestinians or the Black Hats. My money is on the Black Hats."

"Black hats?" Keller asked, a puzzled look on his face.

"The Ultra-Orthodox with their American backers on the right-wing fringe," Stone explained.

Keller still looked puzzled. "So, I don't get it. What's the problem?"

Malik looked angry. "Outside investors means outside muscle making sure that an investment of that magnitude will pay off. The Samaritans may be taking custody of the scroll, but their 'investors' will be there to back them up."

Keller still had questions. "How would the so-called outside investors know what is happening and how could they be in place so fast?"

Malik's face wore a look of grim determination. "I imagine that electronic surveillance of the Samaritans was set up with their assistance and full knowledge. We must assume that they got in place just as we got in place. Whoever **they** are, their goal would be to block any move on our part to obtain the scroll."

Just then the couple with the baby carriage pitched forward and fell from the bench. Even from her lookout post a couple hundred meters from the service door, Stone could see dark stains of blood appearing on their light-colored windbreakers. There was no sound of gunfire, but Stone was on the move immediately, bolting from the ice cream parlor and running toward the hotel exit.

"Abby, where are you going?" Keller yelled, then spotted the *Shin Bet* couple on the ground. "Get down! Stop, for God's sake! You'll get killed." He caught up and tackled her. "You don't have a vest or gun. Stay down." He pulled her to cover at the side of the building.

Stone struggled to break free. "We've got to do something! Let go of me!"

Keller hissed, "You getting killed is not a solution. We need to assess the situation. Did you see anyone come out of the door?"

"No. I saw the door open a crack and the agents fall off the bench." She was panting hard. "We have to help them. Ron, they might still be alive!"

"Not a chance. Whoever put them down is a pro. No noise. Silencer. Two shots." He stared at the door. "The shooters are waiting to see if there is any follow-up action...any agents coming to the rescue." He looked at Abby. "I don't think they saw you bolt from the shop. We need to move carefully down the beach under protective cover. When I'm sure they can't see us from that door, we'll work our way back to the hotel wall. If they don't know we're here, they might still try and use the beach door as their escape route."

"You're going to let them go?" Stone sounded disgusted.

Keller held the gun in front of her. "I have Omar's nine mil, but it only has fifteen in the mag." He aimed his eyes at Abby. "Are you okay?"

"I'm covered in sand. But aside from having the wind knocked out of me by a dumb marine, I'll survive."

Stone started to lift herself up from the ground. Keller pushed her back down. "I said we need to move cautiously, never breaking cover. Our next dash is to that white rowboat ahead of us. Keep low and move as fast as you can. Let's get moving. Where is the professor?"

Keller turned to the ice cream parlor. Malik was standing in the window, looking in their direction, and talking on his cell phone.

"I hope he's made contact with Rafi and Omar. We've got to get off this beach in a hurry."

Keller helped Stone get to a crouching position. "Now," he hissed.

Stone made a dash for the rowboat. Keller was right behind her. Two thoughts entered Keller's mind during the one-hundred-yard dash. First, that Stone ran fast, very fast, track star fast. And second, that he really enjoyed the view of her in motion.

When they reached the rowboat and hunkered down, Keller weighed his options. There was no evidence that they had been observed, no sand kicking up from gunshots, only the sound of the nearby surf at high tide. Looking closely at the beach he noted a number of concrete benches, low walls, and large and formidable sandcastles that could give them a moderately protected path to the wall of the hotel near the service door. His plan was to zig and zag with Stone across the beach from one source of cover to another. After five agonizing minutes, cautiously working their way off the beach, they reached the hotel wall. They flattened themselves against the rough concrete and caught their breath.

Stone was a fast runner, Keller thought, pissed that it took him longer to catch his breath than for Stone to catch hers. "Did you run track or something? You were really moving."

"Field Hockey, right forward. I'm dangerous with a stick in my hand."

"Sorry, I'm not carrying any sticks today." Keller got serious. "We've got to move along this wall toward the door. Stay glued to the wall, behind me. We need to give them as small a target as possible."

"Aye, aye, Sergeant."

"Excuse me, Lieutenant. No disrespect intended." Keller thought it was brave of Stone to show a sense of humor in such a dangerous situation.

Abby hoped the banter helped show she was not afraid. Did Keller think a woman could not be brave in the presence of this kind of threat? "No offense taken. You're the one with urban combat experience. I yield to your expertise in this area."

At that moment, the hotel service door opened wide enough for a gloved hand and black sleeved forearm to be exposed. In the hand was a length of steel pipe a third of a meter in length. Before Keller could process the significance of the pipe, the hand flung the pipe back along the outside of the door in Keller's direction. And then it exploded. Keller disappeared in a cloud of smoke and sand. In the minute it took for the smoke and sand to clear, Stone saw in horror that Keller was lying face down in the sand, motionless. Just then, the service door of the hotel burst open and two people clad in black and heavily armed, looked around and seeing no opposition started to make their escape.

On pure instinct, Stone ran to Keller's body and retrieved the 9-millimeter weapon from the holster on his belt. She racked the gun's slide, then took up a firing stance with the fleeing terrorists in her sights. She squeezed off six quick rounds. Both of her targets went down. Stone kept the gun trained on them, but she needed desperately to go to Keller and see if he was still alive or badly wounded. "Where is the MOSSAD when you need them?" Stone's anger would not let her turn away from the bombers, but she had to know Keller's condition.

BOOK 3: THE BONE BOX (COMING SOON)

Is Keller alive?

Who is really behind the assassination attempts against Stone and Keller?

Will they find the missing scroll before its secret is lost forever?

The search ends in the final book of this series that keeps readers in suspense until the last page. And then they want more. Join us for the conclusion: Search for the Sacred Scroll Book Three: The Bone Box

GLOSSARY

(Words not from Hebrew are noted.)

Abba – Father

Alte kocker – Yiddish, Old man, Idiom - Old Fart

Amah – Unit of length equal to two hand spans

Bavliim – the Babylonians. Singular – *Bavli*

Beit – House. Also, ancestral house, i.e., dynasty as in *Beit David*, the House of David.

Bubbe meises, Yiddish – As used, Grandmother's fables

Cherem - Under the ban of excommunication.

Chevre – Idiom –[My] friends

Cohein - Priest

Cohein Hagadol –Title: The great or high priest.

Dati. Orthodox

Emah – Mommy or mother.

Ephod – A rectangular cloth with a hole cut in the center, worn as an over garment.

Eretz Yisrael. - The Land of Israel. A traditional Jewish way to describe the territory without reference to the modern State of Israel.

Galil – Galilee. Area of Northern Israel from Haifa in the west to the Sea of Galilee in the east.

Genizah – A space set aside in a synagogue or other communal structure for the storage of texts no longer in regular use. These texts contain the sacred name of God.

Giveret – Miss, Ms or Madam.

Habibi – Arabic – My Friend.

Hava Nagilah – Israeli Folk song "Let us rejoice!"

Kibbutzniks – Members of a Kibbutz, an Israeli collective farm.

Kippa – curved dome. Common usage is skull cap.

Kaddish – A prayer recited in memory of the departed

Mazal –Hebrew – Planet. Idiom-Luck

Melekh Shomron – King of Samaria.

Mezuzzah – Doorpost. A box or small carved niche affixed to the doorpost containing scriptural passages.

*Migbaha*t – conical headdress of the priesthood.

Mishegas – Yiddish - Craziness.

Mishkan – Dwelling. The Biblical Tabernacle of the Israelites in the wilderness described in the Book of Exodus

Mossad – The Institute. The Israeli equivalent of the CIA.

Parasang – Unit of distance measure equal to approximately 2.5 miles

Parsa – Persian Unit of measure equal to four miles.

Pehcha – Aramaic/Babylonian title of government official

Sabra –Lit. a prickly pear cactus, idiom used to denote native-born Israelis.

S'gan – assistant. The full term is sgan l'cohein hagadol - the assistant to the High Priest.

Sefer Torat Moshe – Scroll of the Teaching, or revelation of Moses.

Shammes – The server. Person designated by synagogue leadership to attend to the maintenance of the synagogue and its contents.

Sharav – The name of a strong wind that comes out of the Arabian desert.

Sheol – Place name for the dwelling place of the dead.

Shin Bet – An abbreviation for two letters, SHIN and BET which stand for SHIRUTEI BITACHON - security service. This is an arm of the Israeli Ministry of Defense charged with the prevention of terrorist attacks on Israeli soil.

Shomronim – Samaritans

Sofer – Scribe.

Tallit – Fringed garment. Sometimes referred to as a prayer shawl.

Tuches – ass - Yiddish from the Hebrew Tachat, lit. below or bottom.

Yasher koach- "Straight is [your] strength." Idiom –Well done.

Yeshiva Bochers – Yiddish/Hebrew phrase for rabbinical students.

DEAR READER

Over the course of forty-nine years of teaching the Hebrew Scriptures, my students asked tough questions over and over again. *Search for the Sacred Scroll* began as an effort to answer these questions. Thanks to them, it became a labor of love. The creation of the Torah did not have to take place as I have imagined, but it could have.

This book is a work of fiction. The discovery, in Iraq, of an ancient text older than the Dead Sea Scrolls never happened. But the scholarly consensus that the original text of the Torah, the first five books of the Hebrew Scriptures, is a human invention, is very real. Over the last four hundred years, prominent Bible scholars and religious skeptics alike have become convinced that the Hebrew Scriptures, including the Torah, is actually a library. The library contains numerous works, the literary traditions of a people from a particular place and time. This historical novel seeks to provide answers to two questions raised by the existence of the Hebrew Scriptures. How did that unique library actually come to be? Why?

Eliezer and Zadok are fictional characters. Motivations, thoughts, and emotions are rare in Biblical narratives. The process of imagining what is "between the lines" in the Biblical text is known as *midrash*. This is the inspiration for the story of Eliezer, Zadok, and their descendants.

The prophet/priest, Ezekiel ben Buzi, is a real Biblical prophet and priest who lived at the time of the beginning of the Babylonian Exile. There is evidence that he was indeed a religious leader of the Judeans at that time.

The storage of religious documents in a *genizah* is a real custom of some Jewish congregations. The *genizah* in the al Jolan district of Fallujah is fiction. The ancient name of Fallujah, Pumbedita, is fact. Pumbedita was indeed a center of Jewish life and culture in ancient Mesopotamia.

My goal is to pique curiosity into our past. I hope you will want to learn more as you join me on this adventure.

Thank you,
Mark Leslie Shook
St. Louis, Missouri

ACKNOWLEDGMENTS

Composing fiction or non-fiction has been greatly enhanced by word processing programs. Re-writing and making corrections result in multiple versions of the same work. **Samantha Wendling** has helped me to keep these versions straight in the Cloud. Thank you, Sam for providing great computer technical support throughout this project, including clever graphic design ideas for the cover of Book Two.

In this era of satellite imagery, knowing where we are at any given moment on the planet has become almost too easy. But GPS cannot help us follow a journey between ancient locations as experienced 2,500 years ago. To do that requires maps. Thank you, Cartographer Matthew Thomas for your expertise.

Mere words cannot express my gratitude to the Saturday Morning Bible Class of Congregation Temple Israel in St. Louis, Missouri. Each week, for twenty-five years, they have asked great questions. Their love for the Biblical text and its history has inspired and energized me.

For the past twenty years, the nearly 800 students who have endured my teaching of Philosophy 348/349 at Saint Louis University helped to broaden my perspective. I thank them for their patience and diligence. Their questions helped me to hone my answers.

Father Ted Vitali, chair of the Department of Philosophy at Saint Louis University, has provided great support and encouragement. His sense of humor is his secret spiritual weapon. He is a healing metaphysician. He taught me that laughter is non-denominational.

When I began the *Search for the Sacred Scroll* project, I had the broad outlines of the story clear in my head. I did not have control over the little details that add realism to fiction. I engaged a smart and tech-savvy student, **Jerry Thomeczek**, and sent him forth to locate the enriching details. He did a marvelous job and made the single discovery that opened up all sorts of possibilities. He made the historical connection between ancient

Pumbedita and modern Fallujah. The mistakes in the details are all on me. Thank you, Jerry.

My colleague and friend, **Rabbi Jeffrey Stiffman**, actually has distant family members in the Samaritan community. He was kind enough to assist me in gathering materials on the Samaritans now living in Israel. Their part of the story is totally fiction. I thank him for his insights and stories.

Everyone needs someone who looks beyond. This is the person who sees the finished diamond beyond the rough uncut stone. On an impulse, I sent **Rabbi Donald Gerber** some early versions of *Search for the Sacred Scroll*. His unbridled enthusiasm, his conviction that this was a book with great potential, kept me going forward. Our editorial conferences on the deck of a swimming pool in Palm Desert, California, gave me the sounding board I needed when plot dilemmas emerged. That made all the difference. Thank you, Don.

Thank you to Matthew Thomas for the gorgeous maps at the beginning of this book.

I am exceedingly grateful to Keith Newhouse of Newhouse Creative Group for taking this book under his wing and giving me his talented and irrepressible father, Mark Newhouse as my editor. The back and forth between Mark and I has been both frustrating and exhilarating. His patience is boundless. His wisdom is priceless. I have learned so much, so far, and look forward to a fruitful collaboration in the time ahead.

Finally, to Carol, my loving partner and wife of fifty-five years: Thank you for being my support and steady hand through all of the ups and downs of this project. I love you.

MLS

SOURCES

My teacher, **Rabbi Chanan Brichto** (may his memory be for a blessing), taught me to see the text of the Torah as a masterpiece of editing and storytelling. I hear his voice while I am teaching, asking profound questions about the authors of Torah. There are other sources that provided inspiration and material for The Ezra Scroll as well. I list them here:

Akenson, Donald Harmon, *Surpassing Wonder: The Invention of the Bible and the Talmuds*, Harcourt Brace and Co. 1998.

Anderson, Robert T and Giles, *The Keepers: An Introduction to the History and Culture of the Samaritans*, Hendrickson Publishers Inc., Massachusetts, 2002.

Demsky, Aaron, "Who Came First, Ezra or Nehemiah? The Synchronistic Approach," Hebrew Union College Annual, Vol. XLV 1994.

Mantel, Hugo, "The Dichotomy of Judaism During the Second Temple," HUC Annual, Vol. XLIV 1973.

Morgenstern, Julian, "Jerusalem 485 BCE," HUC Annual, Vol. XXVII, 1956.

Rom-Shiloni, Dalit, "Ezekiel and the Voice of the Exiles and Constructor of Exilic Ideology, HUC Annual Vol.

Rom-Shiloni, Dalit, *Exclusive Inclusivity: Identity Conflicts Between The Exiles and the Ones Who Remained*, Continuum 2012.

Inspiring the readers and writers of today and tomorrow!

FREE Book for Subscribing to The NCG Narrative

Subscribe to our free newsletter, The NCG Narrative, to immediately receive a **FREE** eBook from Newhouse Creative Group.

Be the first to learn about NCG's newest releases, get behind the scenes of NCG, enter NCG Narrative exclusive contests and giveaways, and much more!

Subscribe today at NewhouseCreativeGroup.com

Visit NewhouseCreativeGroup.com for more books and other products from NCG Key and the rest of the Newhouse Creative Group family!

www.ingramcontent.com/pod-product-compliance
Lightning Source LLC
Chambersburg PA
CBHW071322130626
46556CB00004B/1706